THE MULADACH

MELISSA PLANTZ

FIRE and GRACE
Publishing, LLC

Melissa Plantz
FIRE and GRACE Publishing, LLC
fireandgracepublishing.com

Printed in the United States of America
First Printing 2020
First Edition 2020

ISBN: 978-1-7349381-6-6

10 9 8 7 6 5 4 3 2 1

This book is a work of fiction. Names, characters, places, and incidents are the products of the author's imagination or are used fictitiously. Any resemblance to actual events, locales, or persons, living or dead, is entirely coincidental.

Edited by Michelle Areaux
Cover Design by VC Book Cover Design

To My Family,

With Love

PROLOGUE

Gerald Reynolds mouthed a silent prayer in the car. He could barely make out the taillights of the semi in front of him through the pouring rain and darkness. He was tired and desperately needed sleep, but he refused to pull off the highway to find a motel. He wanted – no needed – to get home to Stella and the kids.

That was the last time, he told himself. The last time he would run to help the Society. After two decades, he was done. He wasn't going to hide any more secrets from Stella. Surely, he wasn't the only Seer. He slowed the car down as the semi's brake lights flashed on and off.

And this last one almost killed me, he thought as he pulled the small amulet from around his neck and touched it to his lips. Just as Father Mahon had warned, the demons were stronger. The end times were coming closer. Gerald decided he would call Stephen when he got home and tell him he was out. For good. He didn't want something to go wrong, and Ainsley and Ben to grow up without him. The Leaders would be upset, but they would live.

Gerald Reynolds had too much to lose.

CHAPTER ONE

When I stepped out of my best friend, Molly Hiroto's, black Honda Civic after seven o'clock on a Monday night in October, I already knew I was in trouble. The only two streams of light from my split-entry home shone down on the neat lawn, one from the living room and the other from my nine-year-old brother, Benjamin's room. I considered slipping in through the door downstairs next to the garage, and saying I had been in the den for the past hour, but somehow, I knew that wouldn't fly.

As I opened the front door, the smell of Mom's famous parmesan chicken wafted down the steps followed promptly by her serious voice.

"Ainsley? Is that you?"

I wanted to point out that most burglars wouldn't use a key, but instead I hurried up the steps to the living room and met her as she came out of the kitchen and into the dining area. "Yeah, I'm sorry I didn't call earlier."

Stella Reynolds made a face that showed she was indeed both aggravated with me and relieved I was home safe at the same time. "Well,

I'd appreciate a call when you see you're going to be later than you told me, especially when it's this dark outside."

I tossed my backpack on the floor by my dining room chair and slung my favorite Columbia jacket over the back as Mom went into the kitchen to finish dinner. Ever since Dad's tragic accident two years ago, Mom had made it her business to attach herself to Ben and me. Although she worked from home in her office downstairs, and landed a lucrative four-book contract not two days after the funeral, Stella still found time to constantly smother me, her only daughter, a high school senior, close to my eighteenth birthday.

"Well, how'd it go?" Mom asked, as she made a plate of hot chicken, green beans, and biscuits.

I'd gone straight to the fridge on a quest for the last Dr. Pepper. "How did what go?" I asked, as I emerged victorious with my can.

"The job applications at the mall?" Mom asked, raising an eyebrow.

"Oh, they went well, I guess. We both applied to six places and I talked to the assistant managers at the Buckle clothing store and that busy toy store. Hopefully, someone will call this week for an interview." Mom watched me as I took a long drink of my soda, which made me feel a bit uncomfortable, so I turned on my heel and headed back to the dining area. Mom didn't say too much about my junk food addiction, or the fact that I'd easily gained twenty pounds since Dad died. Honestly, it only slightly annoyed me when I had to buy new clothes. And most of those were stretchy now. Thank God for leggings and tunics.

But, sometimes, Mom looked like she wanted to say something.

She followed me to the table and slid my plate down in front of my place setting. "You'd be fantastic at the toy store. You're so good with kids. But, I didn't know you were wanting to get a job until you texted me today." She pulled her blonde hair up into an insane pineapple bun at the top of her head. One of the few things Mom and I have in common is our thick blonde hair, although I suspect she secretly colors hers now. "My gym is looking for a receptionist. You could work there in the evening and weekends and work out for free." Mom had joined the only gym in town nearly a year ago and only went while Ben and I were in school, but she went an average of four times a week, first thing in the morning.

I flipped the tab on the Dr. Pepper can. "I'll check it out. I figured we could use the extra money. Plus, I'm tired of feeling broke around my friends, especially Molly. I want to save up for a car and insurance payments."

Mom leaned on the opposite chair from me and sighed. "Molly loves you regardless of how much money you have or what you drive. You know that. As for money, I know I seem overly frugal, but with Gerald gone, I need to make sure that my income and his life insurance and social security payments last quite a while. Everything goes into…"

"Savings. I know," I finished the sentence for her and instantly regretted it. Boy, did I know. But, I didn't need to remind her that she was a single parent now. I needed to stop worrying her.

"Well, I took the liberty of printing you out a job application for my gym. You have to give it to them in person though." She handed me a sheet from a stack of papers at the end of the table. Sure enough, it was from The Locklyn Gym.

I nodded my head as Mom called my brother for dinner and within seconds, Ben was running full tilt to the table. "Parmesan chicken! My favorite. Did you make a dessert, too?"

Mom smiled sweetly at Ben. He was such a goofball. And he reminded me so much of Dad with his dark hair and eyes.

"No, I didn't have time. I finished the rough draft of my book today."

"Aww, that's great, Mom," Ben said.

"Thanks. It's only taken me four months," she laughed.

"That's good news, Mom. Congratulations," I said, as Mom grabbed hers and Ben's plates from the kitchen counter. "We should do something to celebrate."

"On a Monday night?" Mom asked, scrunching up her nose.

"Yeah, let's get you a cake," Ben chimed in with a mouthful of chicken. "A chocolate cake."

"I could run back out to Food Park. It'd only take a few minutes," I added.

"I don't know," Mom said. "I appreciate the thought guys, but it's awfully dark outside and I don't like you driving in the dark, Ainsley. Anything could happen. You know that."

"Come on, Mom!" Ben pleaded, but I wasn't sure if it was to celebrate Mom's achievement or if he just really wanted that cake.

"Seriously, Mom. It's not like it's ten o'clock at night. I can drive in the dark," I involuntarily closed my eyes as I took a bite of chicken. It was my favorite, too.

Mom laughed and shook her head, but I could tell the thought of celebrating with chocolate cake, one that she didn't bake, sounded pretty good right now. "All right, I'll tell you what. You two help me clean the kitchen after dinner – quickly – and Ainsley can run out for a small cake."

Ben stood up and fist-pumped the air in a celebratory dance.

"You're a goofball," I said to him.

Although chocolate cake sounded pretty good to me, too.

~ ~ ~

After the kitchen was cleaned, I quickly braided my long hair and draped it over my shoulder, threw my jacket on and headed downstairs to the garage.

"Get a big chocolate cake, Ains!" Ben called down the railing.

"No," Mom yelled down next. "A small one is fine. We don't need leftover cake." For some reason I felt that last comment was for me, but I was probably wrong. Mom might smother me at times, but she wasn't into setting her children's self-esteem on fire.

I pressed the buttons to start Mom's Mazda and raise the garage door. Mom was right; the Daylight Savings Time change made it seem later.

And somehow darker.

I had to admit, I loved the replacement car. It was in an Eternal Blue Mica color with black leather interior and happened to be the perfect size for our family.

What was left of our family.

As I pulled out onto our street, I couldn't help but chide myself for being selfish. Mom was trying hard to juggle everything. Dad's car was rear-ended late one rainy night on the interstate on his way back from a business trip, causing his car to slam into the semi in front of him. He'd hovered in a coma for two days before the doctors decided he was clinically brain dead. He would never wake up.

After the insurance company replaced Dad's car with this one, Mom had sold her Nissan to keep the insurance premiums low. She lived frugally and thus, we did too.

"Enough. Get it together, Ainsley," I mumbled. Those thoughts made me feel worse; angry at Dad for dying, guilty for feeling that way and causing Mom to worry, and bitter toward Mom for smothering my every move.

None of it would bring him back. Daddy's little girl needed to grow up.

The drive was uneventful as I suspected it would be. It didn't take long to cross town to the only grocery store. I parked the car and took a quick look in the visor mirror. The bags forming under my eyes told me to go to bed soon. It'd been a long day between the Science test in Mr. Dorchester's class and trying to make a good impression with potential employers at the mall.

As I walked across the parking lot, I thought about calling Molly, but decided it was getting kind of late. She was probably tired, too.

A woman and her toddler passed me on my way through the automatic doors. The mother was pushing her heavy cart loaded down with tons of groceries as her daughter sucked on a lollipop. I smiled at the girl, but when she smiled back, she dropped her half-eaten sucker on the ground and began wailing as only a two-year-old can.

"Oh no, sweetie," her mother calmly consoled her. "Let's go home. I think you're tired." However, the girl only turned her wails up an octave.

I suddenly remembered my purse. "Oh, wait," I said to the girl's mother, who was clearly tired and wanted to go home. "I picked this up at the mall today. Can she have it?" It was a small board book about bears the local toy shop had given away and I'd accepted it on a whim.

The mother hesitated, then nodded her head with a smile. The girl stopped screaming immediately as her eyes grew wide and she took the book.

"Thank you," the exasperated mother said to me.

"Oh, you're welcome. I happened to have it from the toy store."

"Pwincess," the girl called out as she pointed at me.

The mother laughed, "It's your hair. I think it reminds her of that ice princess from that movie."

"Oh, thank you!" I said to the little girl, who melted my heart with her big smile.

She crinkled her little index finger at me, so I bent down as I figured she wanted to say thank you for herself.

"Don't go in there," she whispered.

"Why?"

"Monsters, Pwincess."

Her mother laughed. "Boy is she ever tired. I need to get her home. Thanks for the book, Hun."

"Good night." I waved at the girl who waved back as I continued walking into the store.

I walked to the very back to the bakery. As I stood perusing all of the cakes, cupcakes, and pies and trying to keep in mind that I was there for *one* small chocolate cake, I felt someone looking in my direction. I glanced around expecting to see a lone shopper or employee, but no one was around. As a matter of fact, the entire bakery and deli section was empty.

I turned my ever-growing paranoid self back to the cake display and finally chose a small German Chocolate cake marked down to $4.99. Mom would be proud. Anything more and she might have a fit. Frugality was the word of the decade. I caught a glimpse of my reflection in the mirror above the baked goods. Well, I certainly didn't look like a "pwincess" tonight in my opinion. I could see dark circles forming under my eyes. I needed to get to bed.

As I made my way to the front of the store, I slowed down near the pepperoni rolls. They smelled freshly baked although, in truth, they'd probably been under the heat lamp for a few hours, if not all day. After a brief war inside my head, I moved on.

This urge for sugar and carbs was getting out of hand.

Up ahead, I heard the snarling of a dog, but I couldn't see anyone. Had someone brought their service dog into the store? Maybe a stray had wandered in through the automatic doors. I walked a little faster.

Until I passed Aisle Eight.

I stopped and took two steps backwards. I'd seen something down the household cleaning aisle.

An excruciatingly skinny blonde woman in jeans and a tank stood about halfway down the aisle in front of the air fresheners. Her arms hung limply at her sides and her head was cocked to the right as she stared open-mouthed at the room fragrance display. As strange as the woman appeared, she wasn't the reason my heart skipped a beat. Something was beside her. It stood on two legs as if whispering into the woman's ear. The sounds were a cross between a growl and a language I'd never heard before.

When my brain regained control of my body, I let out an involuntary gasp. The creature snapped back away from the woman and landed on all fours behind her; its skin pulled tight over bulging muscles. It moved around her like a large canine protecting its territory, snarling and baring its teeth. Saliva dripped from its mouth onto the floor as its eyes took me in, reflecting the overhead lights.

The creature bolted towards me.

I turned, vaguely aware I'd dropped Mom's cake, and took off in a run straight into a large carousel. The weight from the heavy turn style filled with books pulled me down as we hit the concrete floor with a thud. I scrambled out from underneath the mountain to get away from the monster, as a Food Park employee grabbed my arm and steadied me.

"Run!" I screamed at the man, and pointed in the direction of Aisle Eight. But there was nothing there. It was gone. I spun in every direction. Where did it go?

"Didn't you see it?" I asked the employee, who was staring at me, probably wondering if he should call the cops. "It, *something*, was down that aisle. It ran at me."

The skinny blonde woman now stood at the end of the aisle with her hand resting on a box of Little Debbie cakes. She must've heard the commotion. How could she not?

"Nah, I was the only one down that way," she said, as she ran her hands up and down her bare arms and jerked her head in the direction of the aisle. Her accent wasn't from around here. She sounded more like she'd come down from a holler somewhere. I noticed the tattoo on her upper arm of a rose entwined with a cross. It was pretty, but the woman had to be chilled. This was October after all.

I shook my head to clear my thoughts.

"It was right beside you. Didn't you hear it talking to you? Didn't you hear it snarling?" I asked the woman, but again, she shook her head.

"Sweetie, there ain't nothin' there. Let alone someone talkin' to me while I picked out my Febreze."

The Food Park employee picked up the now-ruined cake and made a face at the display of books. "I don't know what you saw, if anything, but if you're done shopping, I think you should leave."

I stared at them.

"I need to buy a cake for my mother," I said. I turned and hurried back to the bakery for another German Chocolate cake.

I swallowed hard. There was always a higher price to pay.

CHAPTER TWO

My mind reeled as I drove home. All I could see was that creature lunging towards me. I knew I hadn't made it up, despite what the Food Park employees and that woman thought.

I pulled carefully into the garage and turned off the engine as the garage door closed silently behind me, but I didn't get out right away. Instead, I tapped my fingers on the steering wheel. That creature was large and gray. Almost like a man, but not.

Like a bodybuilder trapped in a gargoyle's body.

I shivered as I got out of the car when I remembered the creature's eyes. They sparkled like a silver sheen of glass. As it'd lunged for me, I'd seen my own reflection for an instant. The thing had mirrors for eyes.

It had run toward me like an animal, but much larger than any animal I'd ever seen not housed in a zoo. It had to have weighed a couple of hundred pounds.

No, I wasn't crazy. Yet, the woman swore she never saw an animal, and the employees acted as if I'd made the whole thing up. Why would I? I guess I was lucky they didn't call the cops or throw me out over the smashed cake and the book display.

They didn't even ask if I was hurt, although I wasn't. Except for maybe my pride.

I did notice as I walked through the lower level of the house, my right knee felt a bit sore. Probably from where I'd turned so quickly to get away from the creature. It'd been a while since I'd ran. I'd stopped playing sports after Dad died and treated every gym class as torture.

Downstairs was quiet. The only rooms down here were Mom's office, the laundry room with a half bath, and Dad's favorite, the family room. However, we spent most of our time upstairs in the living room, kitchen, our bedrooms, or on the wrap-around back deck.

As my foot hit the first stair, Ben bounded down to the landing at the front door. "Ains! What took you so long? Did you get the cake?"

I handed him the cake and he ran to the kitchen. I heard Mom tell him to wait and not slice it on his own.

I entered the kitchen in time to see Mom placing the slices of cake on saucers.

"Ooh, this looks delicious. Thank you, guys for talking me into it," Mom said, and gave Ben a quick hug. He grabbed his plate and headed for the table.

I nodded. "Of course, Mom. Hey, don't cut me a piece right now. I have a headache. I think I'm going to take some ibuprofen and go to bed."

"Are you sure? I hope you're not coming down with something." She reached over and placed her cool hand on my forehead.

"No, I think I'm just tired. It's been a long day. Save me a piece for tomorrow." I hurried out of the kitchen and down the hall to my room before Mom could say anything more.

Once in my room with the door securely shut and locked, I grabbed a water bottle from my nightstand and went straight to my bathroom. I hadn't lied to Mom. I did have a headache. A gargantuan headache. I popped two ibuprofens in my mouth from the medicine cabinet above the sink and took a large gulp of water.

I wanted, no, needed, to tell someone about tonight. But, there was no way Mom would understand, let alone believe I'd seen a creature from the scariest horror movie ever. Even though Mom writes horror novels for a living now.

I slipped out of my clothes and grabbed a pair of pajamas and climbed into bed, but knew it would be a long time before I could finally let my thoughts go. Was Molly still up? As my best friend, she had an obligation to believe me and to not think I was crazy.

Three minutes later, I was on the phone with Molly as she laughed hysterically in my ear. "Well, you are officially crazy," she quipped.

"Seriously, Mol. I did see something."

"Did you tell your mom?"

"No. If I tell Mom then she'll assume I'm going crazy, probably due to Dad and make me see a psychiatrist or something." I turned over onto my back and stared up at the dust bunny hanging off my ceiling. "She's got enough to worry about."

"Okay, so if you saw this thing, what do you think it was?"

I'd already described the grotesque creature to Molly in detail. "I have no idea, but it was definitely not human. It was whispering something to that woman, but she denied she heard anything. I don't know."

"Hmm. Well, it's getting late and we've got school in the morning. I'm going to bed," Molly yawned in my ear.

"I don't know if I can sleep at all tonight."

"Then maybe try Googling "scary creatures in suburbia" and see what pops up. Maybe you're not the only one to see it. But, honestly, Ainsley, you're probably overly stressed with school and your mom…and the anniversary of your dad's passing coming up. Think about talking to Ms. Bell tomorrow. She'd probably agree."

Molly was right. Dad's two-year anniversary since his death was coming quickly and with me feeling responsible for Ben and wanting to take on the added pressure of an after-school job…maybe, it would do me good to speak to Ms. Bell at school tomorrow. She was the psychology teacher as well as a part-time counselor.

"Okay, I'll try to get some sleep. You still picking me up in the morning?"

"Of course. Six forty-five. Be ready, chick." And with that, Molly was off the phone.

I flipped the light on the nightstand off and pulled the comforter up to my face as I'm one of those people who is always cold, especially at night, and so I wrapped myself up like a burrito. I pity the man I marry someday.

I closed my eyes, but I could only see that creature in my head. I was too wired to sleep. If only I could draw, I could sketch the creature to show Molly. Instead, I untangled myself from the cocoon of blanket and grabbed my laptop off the desk, and almost knocked the picture of Dad over. I barely caught the wooden frame. It was a picture of us taken the summer before his accident during our beach vacation. We were sitting side by side on the pier. Dad's arm wrapped around my neck as Mom took the pic. I could vividly remember the roughness of his beard against my face, but I hadn't minded. The picture-version of Dad smiled back at me. Even his dark eyes smiled. He wore a muscle shirt and his ever-present silver medallion with the strange image of a horse with two riders on one side and his initials on the other. He'd been tan and active and fit his whole life. Maybe that's why Mom started her health quest after he died, a sort of living tribute. I put the picture back and climbed onto the bed with my computer.

Once I'd fired it up, I started Googling creatures using clever descriptions like "big gray creatures" and "large mythological monsters" but these search words only brought up images of dragons and the Lochness Monster as well as beasts of all kinds. I needed to narrow the search down further. There was no way the great and mighty Internet didn't have something on this creature.

Unless I *had* completely imagined it. What *if* no one had ever seen anything like it before in the whole world? Did that mean it didn't exist at all except in my head?

I checked the clock. It read 10:38.

Ben should be in bed and probably Mom, too. I got up and opened the bedroom door. Mom's bedroom door across the hall was shut. She was in bed.

I quietly crept down the hall past Ben's room and the bathroom to the kitchen. The house was super quiet which always seemed eerie when you got up in the middle of the night. Almost as if life ceased to exist after everyone went to sleep.

I turned on the Keurig and got down a mug as stealthily as I could. Mom had stopped buying creamer when she joined the gym because she didn't want the added sugar and chemicals, so now my only option for a creamy cup of coffee was stevia and unsweetened cashew milk.

Yum.

When my coffee finished, I grabbed a slice of cake and headed back to my room. I would search for the creature under "big gray demons" next.

Six hours later, I was ready to give up. I'd spent the entire night looking at images of gargoyles, beasts, demons, and Nephilim, and not one matched what I had seen. I'd eaten two slices of cake and drank two cups of coffee, too. Good news though my headache was gone.

I talked myself into one more page of images with the final search of "evil silver colored creatures" when suddenly I saw it. The rendering was as close to what I'd seen than any of the others. Unlike the other images, this one didn't have wings, but did have a horribly scary open mouth filled with razor-sharp teeth. Its build was otherworldly, not human, not animal and was grayish silver in color. The image only showed its profile, but I could imagine what its eyes would look like if the artist had painted them.

I clicked the image and saved it to my computer and then printed a copy. The printer on my desk made a terrible whining noise and I prayed it didn't wake Mom. After it was done printing and using a ton of ink, I clicked through to the artist's website.

Elijah Moore, a student at Queens University in Charlotte was the artist. He only lived one hour from me. The site didn't include a picture of Elijah Moore, but it did come with a contact form. I filled out the form with my cell number and email address and congratulated him on the piece. I asked if he would be willing to speak with me over the phone about this specific artwork entitled "Demon". His other works were creepy, but this was the only one that matched what I'd seen.

I hit send. I knew I was taking a huge risk. This guy could be a pervert or murderer, but so far, he was the only lead I had to proving the creature did exist. If Elijah says he imagined the creature slash demon for his art piece, then that would prove Molly right. I'd boarded the crazy train.

The next morning, as in one hour later, was brutal. I'd slept deep for that one hour and then had to jump up, shower, and dress for school. When Molly honked the horn, I emerged from the house in sweats, a hoodie, messy bun, and a traveler mug of coffee. My sunglasses were as big as my face as I tried to hide the dark circles and puffiness. Makeup would only go so far.

"I take it you had a rough night, Beautiful," Molly said, as I got in the car.

"Ugh, I didn't go to sleep until almost five."

Molly pulled the car away from the curb and I gritted my teeth. I was still convinced that whoever had given Molly her driver's license had been bribed by her father, the orthopedic surgeon.

"Anyway," I pulled the printed copy of Elijah Moore's painting from my bag, "look what I found."

Molly glanced at the picture. "Where did you get that?"

"I kept searching until I found it. This is what I saw. I'm sure of it."

She took another look. "It's a painting. Are you sure you haven't seen it before and somehow imagined it in the store? That painting doesn't make the creature real."

"I'd remember seeing this. It's terrifying. Anyway, I emailed the artist to see if he will talk to me about it. I want to see if he dreamt this thing up or if he saw something that influenced the artwork. He's a student at Queens."

"Are you insane?" Molly pulled the car over as an elderly man honked his horn at us for her suddenly braking without warning. Molly waved in his direction and made a face before turning her natural I-don't-need-to-wear-makeup-because-I-have-a-perfect-olive-complexion face toward me. "You contacted some cat you don't know about a painting he created that you think might be a real creature? He could be a serial killer, Ainsley!"

"Calm down, Mom," I said, as she pulled the car back onto the road without warning the other drivers. "It's going to be fine. I asked him to call or email me, not to meet me at home."

Molly appeared unconvinced. "I'm your best friend. I worry. That's part of the BFF package. Will you at least do me a favor and see Ms. Bell at school?"

"I plan to, but she's a teacher and a counselor, Mol. She's not a psychiatrist."

"Even better. You're less likely to wind up in a padded cell."

Ms. Bell's Psych class was my fourth period before lunch, but I could hardly concentrate. Not in any of my classes all morning and not because I was dead-dog tired. As of the end of fourth period, Elijah Moore had still not called or emailed me. Of course, he probably had classes all day himself or he thought I was a scam of some sort. There seemed to be a million scams in my inbox.

When the bell rang, and the class dismissed for lunch, I walked to Ms. Bell's desk. The redhead from West Virginia was tall, slender, and fit like Mom and about the same age. The only distinguishable difference between Mom and the teacher was that Ms. Bell liked to wear clothes that bordered on the inappropriate level. Nothing too immodest, but she wasn't afraid to show some skin. Apparently, this was okay for high school teachers because the administration had never complained as far as I knew. Neither did the boys in her classes. I liked her because she had a dry sense of humor and made class fun.

"Ainsley, everything, all right? You were awfully quiet today," Ms. Bell asked, in a heavy twang as she glanced at me through her lashes. Maybe this morning wasn't the best day to approach her as I looked like I'd spent a total of twenty minutes getting ready. Which wasn't far from the truth. At least I'd showered.

I should have thought this through. Darn that Molly.

"Ainsley, do you have a question? About class? Or, hair-styling tips?" Ms. Bell asked, as she wrinkled the little spot between her perfectly arched brows. Did she draw those on or were they threaded? I shook my head.

"Um, yes, Ms. Bell. I guess I do have a question. A friend of mine thinks she saw something yesterday. Something no one else saw in the vicinity."

"You mean, a hallucination?"

"Maybe, but my friend's not sick and she doesn't do drugs or drink. It's nothing like that. There's no reason she would have a hallucination. She swears it felt real. As real as you and me."

Ms. Bell sat down at her desk in deep thought as if considering my words. At least she's taking me seriously. Hopefully.

"What is it your friend saw?"

I sat down at the desk across from her, so I could see her eye-to-eye. "She was in the grocery store and walked past an aisle when she saw something resembling a creature standing next to a woman. The creature was as large as a man but wasn't human. It was a grayish silver color. When it noticed her, it charged towards her, but then disappeared."

"And no one else saw this creature but your friend?"

"Yes, only she saw it."

"What about the woman?"

"She denied seeing or hearing anything."

Ms. Bell tapped her fingers on her desk. "She told you this creature was as large as a man, but not a man. Did she describe it further?"

"She could hear it whispering to the woman. It resembled a gargoyle but without wings and its eyes were reflective like a mirror. I thought maybe you could help me to explain to my friend that she's not crazy. Or, at least rule that out," I let out a little laugh.

Ms. Bell smiled. "Well, without meeting your friend, I can't say for sure what she saw or if she did indeed hallucinate. Is she under a lot of stress?"

"Probably the same as everyone else," I lied. Why stop now? I appeared to be on a roll with "my friend's" diagnosis.

"How is her home life?"

"Her mother is a bit on the smothering end."

"And her father?"

"He's no longer living…in the house," I admitted, as I involuntarily winced.

Ms. Bell studied me intently until I felt every bit as uncomfortable as I should. What was I doing? Why didn't I just tell her it was me? Did she think I was making the story up about the creature?

"Here's what I can do to help your friend," she said, as she grabbed her stack of sticky notes and tore one off. She scribbled something on it and passed it to me. "If your friend feels like talking to me, she can either call me at that number or email me at that address. It might help if she documents what she saw then and in the future."

"Do you think she'll see it again?" I asked, as I stuck Ms. Bell's note in my binder.

Ms. Bell stared out the window before she answered. "I can almost guarantee it."

~ ~ ~

I hurried out of Ms. Bell's classroom to find Molly in the cafeteria.

Molly sat at our usual table with our other friends. We always ate lunch with Chris, Maxie, Bronwyn, and Derek. I grabbed a tray and filled it with food from the salad bar and picked a bottle of water. I needed to make better choices today. So far, I'd only had coffee. By the time I sat down, everyone was pretty much done eating except for Maxie and Molly who were in deep conversation about something. Their trays set barely touched.

"Where have you been?" Derek asked. He was by far the cutest boy in school, but totally off limits. He was dating Bronwyn and she was territorial. She'd once jumped all over Molly for sharing a science book with Derek because she thought they were sitting too close together in class.

"I needed to ask Ms. Bell a couple questions about the next Psych test," I answered, shoveling my salad in my mouth to keep any more lies from spilling out. And I was starving.

"Oh yeah," Molly said, raising an eyebrow. "How'd that go?"

"Better than I thought. We can talk about it on the way home."

The last thing I wanted to do was tell our other friends about the creature. I'd be the laughing stock of the entire high school. Way worse than the guy who dresses up as our school Mascot, Craig the Crab.

I ate my lunch quietly as I considered Ms. Bell's comments. She expected me, I mean, *my friend*, to hallucinate the creature in the future. Was that typical?

My phone vibrated across the table. Derek reached for it, but I snatched it up and smacked the tattoo of a snake on his forearm. I didn't have time for a high school senior boy's game. The screen showed it was an unknown number. Normally, I'd let those go to voicemail. Not today.

"Is that your new guy?" Derek teased, as Bronwyn hugged him and smiled at me. Everyone knew I hadn't dated anyone for the last two years.

"Maybe it is. You don't know," I retorted.

I jumped off my seat and took off through the side door before swiping the screen.

"Hi, is this Ainsley Reynolds?" The voice on the other end asked. It sounded like a teenage boy's voice.

"This is she," I answered back, slightly nervous. If this was the artist, he could be a pervert or a serial killer as Molly had so calmly pointed out.

"Ainsley, this is Elijah Moore. You sent me a request to call you about my work."

"Yes, thank you for calling me. I'm specifically interested in your piece titled, "Demon". Where did you get your inspiration for that one?" I asked.

Elijah was quiet for a moment. So quiet, I thought maybe he'd hung up. I glanced at my phone screen to make sure we hadn't disconnected.

"Why do you ask?"

My face grew hot. "It's so different from your other pieces. There's something intriguing about it."

"Well, it's different because it was something my brother described to me. He's not well and he's on medication for various mental disorders. Sometimes he sees things that aren't there. Scary, horrible, demented things. Like the "demon" in the painting. He told me he saw it one day on the train. It was walking around on all fours and whispering to a few of the passengers. Of course, no one else saw it."

"Of course," I answered quietly. "So, he described it to you and you painted your version of it."

"Yeah, he kept talking about it, so I sketched a likeness which he swears is eerily close. I added the paint later."

I hesitated. "Did he happen to say anything about the demon's eyes?" I asked.

"Raymond couldn't see them very well because they reflected the light from the windows on the train. Why are you so interested in my brother's hallucinations?"

"Would it be possible for me to talk with your brother? I know this sounds crazy, but I think I saw something similar yesterday evening. And I don't have a history of hallucinations or delusions. I'm pretty average."

Elijah was quiet again. Finally, he answered, "Raymond was committed to the mental health ward in the local hospital here in Charlotte. I suppose I could meet you there tomorrow and walk you in. But the minute he gets stressed, you have to leave. Understand?"

Before Elijah could change his mind, I confirmed that noon would work for me and I would meet him at the hospital. I'd have to find a way to borrow Mom's car in the middle of the day and skip my classes without getting caught to drive the hour or so to Charlotte.

It'd be well worth the risk of detention to learn exactly what Raymond Moore saw that day on the train.

CHAPTER THREE

After school, I filled Molly in on the conversations with Ms. Bell and Elijah Moore. When I was done, I sat back in the car seat triumphant that come tomorrow I would have the answer to my creature slash demon reality problem.

"You do realize this dude is in the mental health ward of the hospital because he's insane, right? Plus, there is no way I am letting you drive to Charlotte to meet up with this guy and his brother by yourself. I'm going with you."

"It's at least an hour's drive from here. You'd have to miss your classes."

Molly shook her sleek black ponytail so hard, it whipped her in the face. "So, we're seniors. I can sign myself out and tell them I'm sick. Or better yet, I can just be "sick" in the morning and not go at all. Both my parents work all day tomorrow, so they won't know, and I'll be back before either one gets home in the evening. We don't have a landline, so they always text or call my cell to check up on me anyway."

"Well, if you don't think you'll get caught. I don't want you to get into trouble. I'll sign out sick tomorrow. They shouldn't question it. I don't think I've ever missed school for being sick. Plus, I have a test in first period, so I have to show up for that." It was a sad fact that school had been my only constant since Dad died with assignments and classes, and hanging out with my friends, especially Molly.

"Okay, then I'll pick you up at ten at the gas station on the corner. That should give us plenty of time to make it there and meet up with this Elijah Moore."

Molly drove me home and waited while I got dressed, so she could drop me off at the gym. She insisted that she wait outside while I dropped off the application I'd filled out during Spanish. So far, none of the other stores I'd applied to had called. I didn't really want to work at the gym, but I'd promised Mom I would at least turn it in. Even so, I wasn't about to go in there looking as if I'd slept for only an hour last night.

There weren't very many people in the gym when I walked in and I was thankful. In this place, I did feel self-conscious. The few bodies moving around in here today must've been lifting weights and working out for years. I couldn't see one jiggly bit anywhere.

I stood awkwardly at the empty front counter. After about two minutes, I started looking around the room for an employee. Everyone was working out in their own little worlds. Maybe the employee was in the bathroom? As I waited, I caught a glimpse of myself in the mirrored wall that ran the length of the gym. Honestly, I didn't think I looked too bad. I'd been dressing down since Dad died because it was easier for me to deal alone than attracting attention from people. Some days I just wanted to blend in. Disappear. Sure, I was a little heavier than last year, but I could still pull off this pair of skinny jeans with my fitted sapphire blue sweater with the cleavage boosting VS bra. I really should try to get back to dressing like I used to. If anything, now I had curves in all the right places.

"Can I help you find something?" I heard a voice behind me, as I froze in my half-turned position checking out my own bum.

Busted.

A man I'd noticed doing chest presses with the barbell was wiping the sweat off his face with a small towel after his set. His arms were beyond ripped. I wondered if they fit into regular shirts with long sleeves.

I cleared my mind quickly. "I wanted to drop off this application," I said, as I tried not to stare. The man got up and walked across to the desk and reached for my paper with his left hand. I couldn't help but stare at the colorful and ornate tattoo sleeve on his forearm. Some people couldn't pull that off, but he looked as if he was born with the design.

"The owner had to step out for a minute, but he's a friend of mine. His name is Henry. I'll make sure he gets it. Is your phone number on here?"

I nodded as the man set my application behind the counter on the desk. He wrote something on a sticky note and stuck it to the paper.

"Great. Thanks," he glanced down at my app. "Ainsley. I'm Alec. I hope you get the job. Henry could use a smiling face in here every day." He smiled and winked, and my body melted into a puddle on the floor. I was sure of it.

He was taller, at least six foot, and probably a little older than me, with dark brown hair and green eyes. And just the right amount of stubble on his face.

"Thanks." I smiled back as I walked out the door to meet up with Molly, thankful I'd taken the time to put on a killer outfit and fixed my hair and makeup. If this guy worked out here all the time, then I would make a fine receptionist.

~ ~ ~

Our local Cub Scout pack meets every Tuesday at the Methodist Church in our small town. Normally Mom would take Ben, but tonight she wasn't feeling well and asked me to drive him.

"It's a Den meeting, not a Pack meeting, so you don't have to stay. I typically drive down to the library and kill time. It's only an hour."

"That's fine, Mom. I have a test to study for anyway. I'll do it at the library."

Ben got dressed, with his shirt, neckerchief and its slide, belt, and hat situated perfectly on himself. It was cute, so I had to take a picture of the enormous goofball before we could leave. Mom still felt sick and made herself a makeshift bed on the couch in the living room as Ben and I headed down to the garage, and after he'd buckled his seatbelt, we drove the ten minutes to the church on the hill.

"Did you bring your Bear handbook?" I asked.

"Yep, and I know the Scout Law and the Scout Oath."

"Really? What are they then?"

Ben held up two fingers and recited both from memory which sounded vaguely familiar, so I was sure he was correct.

"You think Mom is going to be alright, Ainsley?" Ben asked.

I glanced at him through the rearview mirror. "Yeah, Ben. She's just sick. Probably a stomach virus or something going around." This seemed to satisfy him, and he turned his attention to the window. I swallowed. Losing one parent was hard, if he lost both...

When I pulled up at the church, Ben hopped out of the car to head inside. "Hey!" I hollered after him. He turned around, his neckerchief out of place from the wind. "I'll be back in time to get you, so behave and wait for me inside those glass doors."

"Okay, Ains!" He took off into the church.

I drove slowly down the steep hill and pulled out onto the busy road. The library, elementary school, and post office buildings were so close they were visible from the church parking lot. As I pulled the Mazda into a parking space, I noticed movement next door in the elementary school's parking lot. Normally, the school was empty at this time in the evening unless a teacher worked late, but tonight I didn't see any cars in the lot. However, three figures walked awkwardly through the lot headed to the school. Two of the figures were horrifyingly familiar.

I rummaged through my purse and pulled out my cell phone, quickly scanning for the camera icon. Once found, I held the phone up to the windshield and zoomed in on the three figures. The one in the middle was a tall man, but I couldn't make out any features. The camera wouldn't zoom in close enough without losing clarity. I hit record and scanned the other two figures. They were alternating between walking on two legs and on all fours. They were as big as the man.

I dropped the phone and panicked as I tried to locate the camera icon again and turn it on before they disappeared. The three figures were entering the school from the side of the building. I replayed the video, but it was garbled. Worthless. No one would believe me, but I knew it was more of them. More of the creatures from Food Park and no one knew. And they were with a man.

Maybe I needed to get closer.

I turned off the car and got out as I slid the lanyard with the key ring around my neck. Although there were cars parked in the library lot, no one was outside. I didn't bother locking the doors as I didn't want the beeping to somehow alert those creatures to my presence. Was I really this brave? Or, really this crazy?

Elijah Moore's brother believed what he saw was real. *And it landed him in the psych ward*, I told myself as I made my way past the library and over to the school. I got as close to the brick building as possible. I could still see Mom's car in the library parking lot under a street lamp.

When I finally made my way to the corner of the building, I peeked my head around. I could see the steps that led to the basement door. The custodian was probably the only one to ever use the door. With my sudden urge to collect evidence, I crept down the concrete steps. Tonight, the door was unlocked. I peered through the glass but couldn't make anything out. It was too dark. I'd have to go in. I pushed the bar across the handle and pulled the door at the same time. Surprisingly, the door opened the rest of the way silently.

The corridor was empty and dark except for a light flooding into an area at the end of the hall and to the right. I followed the wall to the right with my phone held out in front of me. If I could record the creatures with the man, maybe it would prove they existed. When I got closer to the open doorway, the source of the light, I froze. I heard what sounded like whimpering.

A duo of snarls filled the hall as I heard a man whisper. "I'm sorry that I have to do this, but it'll be wonderful. Eternal." The snarling grew louder. I needed to get a video, but my body froze in fear. I shouldn't be here. Any second now, the pair of creatures could bound out of that room and rip me to shreds.

This last thought freed my legs and I started retreating to the door when I heard something acidic being poured. The crackling and hiss of the acid caused the whimpering to reach a high-pitched scream as I took off to the exit door.

There was someone in that room. They were doing something horrible to someone in that room.

Before I could open the door, the screaming suddenly stopped. It was silent. Trembling, I looked over my shoulder. Nothing. I slipped out and sprinted around the building and across both parking lots to the library's front doors.

Once inside, I tried to tell the librarian at the front desk what I'd seen and heard, but I couldn't catch my breath. Was I really this out of shape?

By the time I could talk, tears streamed down my face. "We have to call the police," I gasped out. "I saw some...some people at the school next door. I think they're hurting someone in the basement," I practically yelled.

The older woman at the counter frowned. "What are you talking about?"

I rolled my eyes and reached for the phone on the desk. "There are some people at the school in the basement and I think they're hurting someone," I repeated.

The woman slid the phone out of my reach as she made a face. "I'll call them, but this better not be a joke."

Something sharp bit into my hand. I raised it to my face and realized my white knuckles still clutched my cell phone. Why hadn't I called 9-1-1 myself? I couldn't even think straight. I stared up at the giant wall clock behind the flustered and hateful librarian. Ben would get out of scouts in forty minutes.

It took the police about thirty minutes to send two police cars out to the elementary school and the library. Apparently, the Principal had been called as two police officers met with him and walked through the building. The other two came inside the library to question me. The librarian didn't seem pleased to have so much drama in her library on a Tuesday evening.

One police officer took my statement. "So, you're stating you saw three figures skulking around the elementary school in the dark and you decided to follow them until you saw them go into the basement?"

I hesitated as I searched my brain for the right words to send to my gaping mouth. I couldn't tell the police that I'd stupidly followed the figures into the building because I thought two of them were demons.

"Yes, that's correct," I answered, and I hoped this was the last fib on this Day of Lies. "Something didn't seem right. Can I go now? My little brother is getting out of Scouts and I have to pick him up. He's only nine."

"Of course. We've got your contact information in case we need to reach you."

I thanked the officer and hurried out to Mom's car as he questioned the librarian next. As I pulled the car onto the road, I observed the police and the Principal standing outside the school building talking calmly and I had a gut feeling they hadn't found any evidence of people or creatures.

Ben's Den leader and a few other parents stood inside the glass doors when I arrived at the church to pick him up. I spent a couple of minutes in small talk with them while I peeked nervously over my shoulder. If the cops hadn't found any evidence, then where did the creatures go? Who was screaming in that basement room?

Ben talked nonstop on the drive home about the meeting and his craft tonight, a glass lantern made from a Mason jar. He'd painted it green and black to resemble Frankenstein's Monster. Perfect for Halloween in a few weeks. The paint was still slightly wet, so he balanced the jar on a paper bag on his lap.

We found Mom in the kitchen making herself a cup of hot cocoa.

"Feeling any better?" I asked her, as I sat my bookbag down on the kitchen counter and went to the fridge to see if we had restocked the Dr. Pepper. Sadly, no.

"A little bit. I don't know what I've come down with, but it's kicked my butt. I have a lot of sinus drainage, so it could be seasonal allergies, I suppose. I plan to take tomorrow off and rest. What is that?" Mom asked Ben, who'd placed his lantern and paper bag on the counter. He was busy making his own hot cocoa with the Keurig. I waited patiently for Ben to fill Mom in on his adventure tonight. I could wait a few minutes before telling her about mine.

When his cocoa was done, I helped him carry it to the dining table, but he decided it was too hot and went to his room to play Fortnite until it cooled enough to drink. Mom carried hers into the living room. I followed her and sat down on the loveseat beside the couch.

I waited until she had made herself comfortable in her little blanket nook before I spoke. "Mom, something happened tonight while Ben was in Scouts," I spoke quietly. I certainly didn't want him to hear any of this. He'd already seen the police cars from the church's parking lot.

Mom's eyes grew wide. "What happened? At Scouts?"

"No, not there. Over at Ben's school. I parked at the library to do my homework, but I saw three...people...skulking through the school's parking lot. They acted suspicious and then they went into the school through the basement door. I went inside the library and called the police."

"Well, thank God, you saw them. Who's to say what they were going to do? Did the police catch them?"

"Not before I left to go back for Ben. The officers took my statement and my contact info, so I wanted to let you know in case they call or stop by over the next few days." There was absolutely no way I was going to tell Mom I'd gone into that building to hunt for creatures.

Mom reached over and kissed the top of my head. "You did the right thing calling the police," she cupped my chin in her hand. "Gerald would be so proud of you and the responsible young woman you've become."

I nodded as Mom resumed her spot on the couch. I gathered my bookbag and a bottle of water and headed to my room.

Yeah. Dad would be super proud of me now.

If only Mom knew.

CHAPTER FOUR

The next morning, I got up earlier to get ready for school since I had to walk. Molly planned to stay home "sick" as we discussed. I'd decided to wait until our drive to Charlotte to tell her about the figures at the school last night.

The walk to school was quick as I stayed lost in my thoughts about the creatures and replayed the sounds from last night repeatedly in my head. I sent up a small prayer for the poor person who'd been in that basement.

I'd stopped at my locker before first period to grab a book when Ms. Bell approached me.

"Good morning, Ainsley. I was hoping to talk with you for a few minutes."

"Actually, I think I'm coming down with something. I'm not feeling very well. My mom was sick last night, so I might go home after this test in first period."

"Oh, okay. Well, I wanted to let you know your friend hasn't reached out to me, yet." Ms. Bell smiled.

"Okay, thanks. I'm sure she's probably trying to figure it out on her own," I answered. Wow. The first true statement I'd uttered all morning.

"I'm sure she is, but if she needs me, she has my info. I'd really like to help her. Hope you feel better," she said, and walked around me to join the throng of students making their way to their first class of the day.

Molly picked me up right at ten o'clock at the gas station to head to Charlotte. She, being the best BFF ever, pulled into the local pizza place drive-through before getting on the interstate and got us both fresh personal pan pizzas and a 20-ounce Dr. Pepper since we wouldn't have time for lunch.

Molly listened as I told her about last night in between my bites of pizza.

"So, you have no idea if they found anything at the school last night?" she asked, as she took a bite of her pizza while keeping her eyes on the highway.

I shook my head. "No, but I think something would have been on the news. Plus, the police would've called with more questions. Maybe they were gone by the time the police got there."

"If there'd been a body, my mom would have received a call last night, I'm sure," Molly remarked, biting her lip, a sure sign she was deep in thought. I'd forgotten her mother worked as lead investigator in the forensics department.

"Could they have seen you?" she asked.

"I don't think so. No one followed me out."

"That doesn't mean they didn't see you streaking across the parking lot."

I thought about it. I couldn't remember if the basement had windows that peered out onto the lot. "Maybe, but I don't think so."

I was thankful when Molly changed the subject to last week's episode of American Horror Story. The remainder of the drive was smooth, although my GPS had us take a few unnecessary turns to get to the hospital's parking garage.

I called Elijah Moore once we'd parked the car. The man was already on the third floor of the hospital waiting for us. We'd agreed that he would meet us at the elevator when we came up. He'd arrived early to prepare his brother for visitors. Whatever that meant.

When the elevator doors opened on the third floor, a handsome young man not much older than us wearing jeans and a Polo shirt, greeted us. Molly let out a small sound of approval as he introduced himself and shook her hand. I stifled a giggle, but didn't let Elijah see me elbow her in the ribs as we followed him down the hall to his brother's room.

"My brother is having a good day and is expecting you. He's right down here in Room 314." When we reached the room, Elijah walked right in, but I hung back a moment to read the nametag on the door.

Raymond Moore.

I followed Molly into the room. Raymond was in his own private room that consisted of a bed, built-in cabinets on the wall, and a television attached opposite. Not much else in his room other than a few trinkets that appeared handmade on the windowsill. One was a green wooden jewelry box with a flattened penny as the handle.

Elijah introduced us to his brother who didn't look at all what I'd pictured. I'd pictured the stereotypical mental patient from the movies, a crazed Jack Nicholson complete with straitjacket. Raymond was probably in his twenties, not much older than his brother I would guess, with his brother's dark hair and piercing blue eyes that sort of matched his royal blue tee shirt. He was sitting up in the bed.

"My brother tells me you think you saw one too." His comment left me speechless. The mental patient was clearly thrilled that I might share in his delusion. I set my apprehension aside and decided to tell this man the truth. He was probably the only person who would understand.

I stepped closer to his bed. "I saw a creature that resembles the one in your brother's painting two nights ago. Then last night, I saw two of them in a parking lot walking with a man."

I could feel Elijah's eyes on me and hoped he wouldn't think I was trying to rile up his brother. I knew I sounded crazy to Elijah, and possibly Molly too at this point. The only confirmed crazy one in the room sat quietly in his bed and smiled.

"Yes, that sounds like them. They whisper to people. Some can hear them, and some can't. Some are entranced by their words and it leads to madness. Others are affected differently."

"Affected differently? How?" I asked.

"You have beautiful hair."

"Thank you," I answered, not sure how to get him back on topic.

"The people who can't see them only hear their voices as their own thoughts. These people go mad and wind up a victim of a suicide or murder. They go willingly to their deaths. The other people who can see and talk to them are influenced to do terrible things."

"What kinds of things?" Molly asked.

"Murder for one."

"How do you know this?" I asked.

"I could see them, and they tried to talk to me. They told me things. What I could do to be famous. How people would remember my name forever. They wanted me to do terrible things, they appealed to my senses, made doing horrible things wonderful in a twisted sort of way. I called them the Muladach because they are, in essence, sorrow and madness." Raymond chewed on his bottom lip as he stared out the only window in the room. "Did you see their eyes?"

"Yes, but only for a moment," I answered.

Raymond leaned forward on the bed. "Their eyes are reflective like mirrors. If you look into them long enough, you can see yourself. Your future self. The person you will be with their help. The evil and terrible, yet also the great and remembered for eternity, version of yourself. I could've been remembered for centuries for the things they wanted me to do. Things that seemed right."

"But you didn't hurt anyone, did you, Raymond?" Elijah interjected. "My brother had himself committed to keep himself and others safe."

"Did it work?" I asked. "Do you feel safe from the creatures, the Muladach?"

Raymond shrugged as he bit at a wayward fingernail. "I don't see the demons in here. At least, not yet. But you should be careful. You've seen them, and I bet they've seen you."

~ ~ ~

Elijah walked us to the parking garage after our visit with Raymond. He'd seemed tired after my questioning, but Elijah was convinced that it wasn't because of me but the medication Raymond was on to control his hallucinations and outbursts. Elijah and Molly walked ahead of me and I noticed the two of them chatted non-stop, and not about Raymond or the Muladach. Was Molly flirting with Elijah Moore?

By the time we got to the front of the garage building, the two had exchanged numbers. I thanked Elijah for allowing me time with his brother.

"No problem. I don't know what it is that you saw, but please remember my brother does have a history of mental illness," he said before he turned to Molly. "Call me if you need anything else."

Molly and I spent the next hour or so theorizing about the creatures and Raymond's alleged hallucinations, and, of course, Elijah.

"What do you think of Elijah?" Molly asked, with the widest grin I'd ever seen plastered on her face.

"Oh, he's hot, Molly. But, he's in college. I doubt your parents are going to let you date him."

"Why not? I'm seventeen and a senior. He's only nineteen. Next year, I might attend Queens. You don't know." Molly made a face at me.

"I know your mom probably knows how to get rid of a body without a trace," I reminded her, and she laughed. She continued talking about her possible future with Elijah Moore for the remainder of the drive back home.

We timed it well so that Molly would drop me off about a block from home, and I would walk the rest of the way to arrive at the house right on time. This way Mom couldn't tell Molly's parents she'd seen her driving around when she was supposed to be sick. I just hoped no one from the school had called Mom after I signed out. Although if Mr. Clendenin, the Vice-Principal, had called, Mom would've texted me by now.

As I approached, I noticed an unfamiliar black SUV parked in front of the house next to the mailbox. Strange. Normally, people visiting the neighbors would either park in their driveways or in front of their homes. However, the street was quiet as most of our neighbors were retired or worked day jobs.

As I unlocked the front door and started inside, I heard Mom's voice carry over the railing, but due to the oversized couch blocking my view, I couldn't see through the bannisters. I quietly stepped up the stairs. Mom sat in the recliner in front of the large picture window while two men sat on the couch. They both stood up when they saw me, but I couldn't tear my eyes away from the more muscular man. It was the man from the gym. The man with the ripped arms. Surprisingly, he *could* fit his arms into a suit jacket.

"Hi, Alec? Did I miss a text or something? Is this an interview for the job?" I smiled my prettiest smile and hoped I didn't have any leftover pizza from the trip back stuck in my teeth. The man from the gym bit his lower lip and I caught the other man glancing questioningly at his friend.

"Ainsley, I'm glad you're home. I was going to call you," Mom said, looking relieved until she realized I'd called the man by his first name. "Do you two know each other?" she asked, as she motioned for me to come over to her. I didn't move. This was weird.

The man from the gym put one hand up as if he were approaching a wild animal and extended his other hand. "Hi, Ainsley. No, the gym doesn't make house calls," he joked, as I reached for his hand to shake it. "I'm *Detective* Alec Graham. This is my partner, Detective David Tudor. We would like to talk to you about what you saw at the elementary school last night."

"Ben's school was on lock-down today," Mom interjected. "I sent him over to Rachel's house next door for now. They found a body at the library."

I sat down heavily on the loveseat. A body at the library. Not at the school.

The half-Detective half-Gym Rat Alec and his partner resumed their seats on the couch. "I know you told the officer everything in your statement yesterday, but can you tell me what happened last night in detail?" Detective Graham asked.

I pulled my backpack off and laid it on the floor beside me as I studied the two men. Detective Tudor was tall and thin, but unremarkable next to his partner. As I stared into Detective Graham's green eyes, I wondered how old he was. He looked too young to be a detective investigating a homicide. At least in my unprofessional opinion.

Why was I thinking about how old he was? There was a body at the library and I witnessed something last night.

"Mom wasn't feeling well yesterday evening, so I took my brother to his Scout meeting. I didn't need to stay, so I drove to the library to study."

Detective Tudor observed his notes for a moment. "The officer reported that when you arrived at the library, you saw three people walking across the lot at the school."

"Yes, I saw three men walking closely together towards the school. They were…" I trailed off. I hadn't told the police about following the men into the building or about the screams. What if the body belonged to the person they were hurting last night? I felt my eyes grow hot as I wanted to burst into tears.

I had to keep it together.

Detective Graham leaned forward on the couch cushion until his arms rested on his knees about a foot from me. "Ainsley, I need you to try to remember everything. It is vitally important. If there is something you forgot to tell the officer last night, that's okay. I know how chaotic things can get. But I need as much information as you can give me."

I stole a glance at Mom, but she caught it. She came over and sat down on the loveseat. "Go on, honey," she urged, as she rubbed my arm.

Telling Alec slash Detective Graham everything would probably get me into trouble with Mom, but someone was dead, and it may have been my fault for not telling sooner.

Detective Tudor had a notebook and pen at the ready but waited for me patiently to bare my soul in front of my mother. I took a deep breath as I made eye contact with the handsome stubbled-faced detective so close I could smell his cologne.

"Last night, when I saw the three, um, figures, I did something stupid and impulsive."

Detective Graham didn't blink. I searched his face, but couldn't read what was going through his mind. His thoughts probably started with *stupid girl.*

"I followed them into the school through the basement door."

"Ainsley!" Mom gasped.

Detective Tudor leaned forward with his notebook, but Detective Graham nodded for me to go on.

"They walked across the parking lot and around the side of the building. I tried to record them with my phone, but it came out blurry and garbled. You couldn't see them. So, I decided to follow them and try to get a better picture. They'd left the basement door unlocked."

I replayed the moment in my mind. The dark hallway. The light streaming out of that room. The vicious snarling. That horrible scream.

My eyes must have glazed over because Detective Graham leaned closer to me. "What did you see, Ainsley?"

"The corridor was dark except for a light that spilled out from a room near the end of the hall. I got as close as I could, but I was afraid they would see me. I could hear someone talking, but it was difficult to make out the words."

"Did you catch any of what they were saying?" Detective Tudor asked.

"Something about eternity. Or maybe, about something being eternal. I think he was apologizing to someone. I heard what sounded like an acid being poured and then someone screamed. I ran. I ran as fast I could to the library and they called the police."

Detective Tudor scribbled furiously into his notebook.

Detective Graham sat back on the couch with his eyes on me as he loosened his necktie as if he needed air. "Do you remember which librarian called the police?" he asked.

"An older woman. She's practically there all the time. At least every time we go it seems. The officer questioned her last night," I paused, as I debated if I should ask the question, and then decided I needed to know. "Who was it?"

"Who?" Detective Graham asked.

"You told us they found a body at the library. Do you know who it was?"

Detective Graham shook his head. "Not yet, but our forensics team is working on identification." He stood up, and Detective Tudor taking his cue, shut his notebook and rose as well.

"Is it alright if we contact Ainsley if we have any more questions?" Detective Graham asked Mom.

"Of course, whatever you need to catch these people."

After the detectives confirmed my cell number, we followed the men to the front door as they thanked us for our cooperation. On the porch, Detective Graham handed me his business card with his contact info. "In case you think of anything else that could help us," he said with a smile. "And no more following suspicious men into buildings. You call for help," he added with a wink.

"Absolutely. Thanks," I answered. He handed Mom a card too. I watched the two men leave in their unmarked SUV.

However, when I shut the front door, Mom sat on the steps with fury written across her face. "I can't believe you lied to me, Ainsley! Why would you follow three men into a dark building? You could have been caught. You could have been killed. That could be your body at the morgue!" Mom was so angry, her words came out in a half-hiss, half-yell.

"I know it was stupid. That's why I didn't tell you last night. Or the police."

Mom shook her head. "Don't lie to me again, Ainsley. With Gerald gone, it's you and me and Ben. I can't protect you when you go places and do things I don't know about."

I stared at the carpet and nodded my head. "May I be excused to my room now?" I asked.

"How do you know that detective?"

"I don't. Not really. I dropped off that application at the gym yesterday and he was there. His friend Henry owns it, but he was out. He said he would give it to him. I think he must go in the afternoons. That's all."

Mom slid over to let me pass. She didn't say another word.

I grabbed my backpack from the living room and went straight to my room. Now was certainly not the time to tell Mom about my trip to Charlotte today or meeting with a mental patient at the hospital to question him about his demon hallucinations. After this, I'd be lucky if Mom let me attend graduation. No need to add to it.

I'd been in my room for a few hours getting caught up on homework when Molly called. She sounded breathless. "Hey, did you see the news?"

"Let me guess. They found a body at the library today?"

"Yes! How did you know?"

"There were two detectives here when I got home. They questioned me about what I saw at the school last night. I told them everything. Mom is furious."

"You told them everything?"

"Well, not about the creatures. I told them about going into the basement. And the screams." I threw myself across the bed. "I take it, you saw it on the news?"

"Mom is working the case. I overheard her tell Dad about the man."

I sat up on the bed. "It was a man's body?"

"Yep. Apparently, it was pretty gruesome. He had giant pieces of his flesh missing. They also cut off his index finger and part of his leg. Mom said there was also a framed piece of art displayed beside his body. At first, she thought it was a painting on canvas and then on closer inspection, she thought it was tacked to leather. But now, she's pretty sure it's the man's flesh. Their waiting on test results, but it appears to her that the killers framed the man's tattoo of a Native American Chief."

My stomach turned.

"Hey, you can't tell anyone. Mom could get fired for telling Dad."

"You know I won't. Mol, do you think that man is who I heard screaming last night?" I got off the bed and went to my bathroom. I might actually get sick over this.

"Maybe, but don't think about it. You told the police and they searched the building. I don't think they found anything at the school. You did your part and now you're out of it. Oh, by the way, Elijah invited us to an art exhibit at Queens University Friday night. Tell me you can go."

"I'll have to check with Mom and tonight is definitely not the night to ask. She's still mad. I haven't even left my room to grab a snack. I'll probably skip dinner unless she calls."

"Okay, well, ask her tomorrow so I can tell Elijah. I don't want to go to Charlotte by myself." I hung up the phone a few minutes later and got into bed. Maybe I would go to bed early tonight. I was sick thinking about that poor man. Realistically, what could I have done? If the creatures or the man had seen me, then I would probably be the dead body at the morgue. Mom was absolutely right about that.

I turned over onto my left side and stared at Dad's picture on my desk. Dad would've known what to do. He'd served as a Marine when he and Mom first got married. He probably would've charged into that school and brought out both creatures and the man. I silently laughed as I wiped away a single tear. They were always escaping out of my eyes when I least expected them.

I turned over onto my right side and stared at my closet door. Alec Graham. He'd stressed the word "detective" when he introduced himself this time. Yet, when he'd given me his card, he'd smiled at me just like he did at the gym. There was something about him. He was so good-looking in a Green Arrow-kind-of-way. I wished I'd told Molly about him. For some reason, I hadn't told her about meeting him briefly at the gym either even with her sitting outside in her car. I'd put his contact info into my phone as soon I'd shut the bedroom door. Just in case, of course.

As I drifted off to sleep, my last thoughts were of the young detective.

~ ~ ~

After school, I ended up walking home because Molly had a dentist appointment. I didn't mind. Fall is my favorite season with its leaves, crisp air, pumpkins, corn mazes, and pumpkin spice lattes. I was definitely one of *those* girls. I was even dressed in my ripped skinny jeans with gray ankle boots and Duke hoodie over a gray and blue baseball tee. The jeans were a little snug, but surprisingly I could wear them again. Living not too far from the beach had its perks. It was windy, but not bitter cold. It was a beautiful day to walk, especially in this neighborhood, Cutter's Street.

Cutter's Street was quiet and full of suburban homes with trees planted along the sidewalks. I had to walk the length to reach my street. It was peaceful as very few kids lived on this street. It used to house a junior high about halfway down, but that was abandoned years ago when the Locklyn Middle School had opened on the other side of town. Even the little market next door to it had closed, although I wondered if the owners still rented out the tiny apartment on top.

I slowed down near the junior high school building. I'd always loved this building. Mom and Dad had both gone to school here. It was a large three-story monolith built not long after the turn of the twentieth century with rectangular wings and an oval structure near the middle that jutted out. I wasn't sure what it was called, maybe a turret, but I would've loved to have taught a class in a room with windows like that. Mom had told me that classes had been taught in that third-floor room, but that the second-floor room had housed the library and the first-floor room was the Principal's office. They didn't make schools like this anymore. At least, not around here anyway.

As I came closer to passing the entrance, I stopped cold as I heard a low humming sound in my ears, like the low roar of a generator but much quieter. I blinked as the view of the sidewalk in front of me shifted as if someone ripped a veil away. The trees, houses, cars, everything vibrated and rippled for a moment. Was I having a stroke or something? Then it stopped. Everything appeared right again until the front door of the abandoned junior high swung open and one of those creatures ran out and across the street. In broad daylight. It disappeared behind a house.

And I was pretty sure it hadn't seen me.

It happened so quickly, I watched as the front door to the old school slowly closed again.

If the creature was a hallucination, then the front door shouldn't have moved. Yet, it did. I glanced over at the houses lining the opposite side of the street. Where had the thing gone? Was there only one this time?

I turned back to the school. What would the creature want in an old abandoned building? I wanted to go inside and investigate while the door was clearly unlocked, but Mom's angry face popped into my mind's eye. Plus, what if the creature came back while I was inside alone?

I grabbed my phone out of my back pocket and pulled up Detective Graham's contact info. What would I tell him? I'd seen another suspicious figure emerge from this building too?

Instead I called Molly. On the third ring, she answered in a hushed voice. I'd forgotten she was at the dentist.

"Molly, I'm at the old junior high on Cutter's Street. I saw another one of those creatures come out of the building and go across the street."

"You didn't go in the school, did you?"

"No, not yet. But I really want to know what's going inside of there."

"Call the police. This isn't your problem," she whispered.

"It's my problem if I'm the only one that can see them. I have to find out what they're doing here. Someone already died because I didn't do something."

"Wait there. I'll be over in a few minutes," Molly said and hung up.

She was definitely a best-friend-forever-kind-of-chick.

I text Mom that I was running errands with Molly and would be home soon. Molly arrived less than ten minutes later. Apparently, she hadn't seen the dentist yet, so she rescheduled.

After looking around to make sure no one was watching, Molly and I slid into the building. She'd brought her tire iron from her car and handed me the can of pepper spray in case we ran into a creature…or a creature of the human variety. We walked through the first floor, peering into the empty classrooms and closets. The daylight streamed in through the windows and highlighted the crumbling murals on the walls. The paint was peeling as the artwork from students past disappeared into time never to be seen by the public again. It was a sad sight.

We didn't find anything on the first floor, so we found a flight of stairs to the second floor. The school was so large it had stairwells at all four corners of the building. There were less classrooms on this floor, but they were larger. The building was built to last with its thick walls and hardwood shelving and floors. We stopped at the room that had once been the library and admired the turret's tall windows. I could imagine the room filled with enormous bookcases and tables. It must have been beautiful once.

We continued down the hall a little further until Molly pulled me into what was probably once the music room. The walls were painted with musical notes. "My dad used to talk about practicing with the band in this room. Yep, there's the musical notes they painted all around the room while he was here. He played the tuba and loved it."

Then she got quiet. "He hated junior high though. He was the only Japanese kid here and my grandparents had immigrated so they only spoke basic English. He was born here, but it didn't matter. He was still bullied."

"Bullies suck. Racist bullies suck more," I said. "Well, he showed them. Look at him now."

Molly nodded and smiled. We headed back out into the hall to the stairwell to climb the steps to the third floor. At the double doors on the top floor, I stopped short.

"Do you feel that?" I asked Molly.

"What?"

"The air up here feels different. Like it has an electrical charge," I whispered.

"It's probably the asbestos we're breathing in. This place has been closed for years."

I peered in through the small windows of one of the doors. This floor seemed much smaller. I jumped as Molly opened the other door.

"Come on, Scaredy Cat."

As I followed Molly, I was more apprehensive about this floor. My gut told me to be on guard. This felt different. We stopped at the end of the hall. There was a classroom to our immediate right, but further down the hall was another classroom to the right and another one at the end. Lockers lined the wall on the left. Less rooms for something to hide up here. I listened intently. Nothing, but the sound of Molly's footsteps as she walked into the room on the right. The floorboards creaked as we surveyed the room with its wooden desks and empty counters where sinks must have previously set. This must have been a science classroom.

We turned and headed for the middle classroom. The hallway was darker up here with less windows, but the middle classroom had plenty of sunlight from the tall windows that ran floor to ceiling, especially from the turret. As I expected, it took my breath away as I stood in the doorway and Molly walked inside. The cabinets were built into the walls and a large island with shelves underneath jutted out into the center of the room. The walls were covered with decaying murals. "This was the Art Room," I observed.

"Yeah, it's as Dad described it. The teacher kept desks on both sides of this island and he would stand over there near the windows, so everyone could see him while he…" she pointed to the half-circular wall of windows but stopped mid-sentence. I walked over and stood beside her as I followed her gaze.

Until I realized she wasn't pointing at the tall windows after all, but at the body lying on the classroom floor.

~ ~ ~

Molly and I stood over the body for a few moments before she took out her cell phone and called 9-1-1. A crazy part of me wanted to protest that our parents would find out we were here in this abandoned building and we would be in trouble. But, this was a dead body. We had to report it.

A real dead body and not embalmed. I'd seen bodies before at funerals, and of course, I was with Dad when they removed his life support. However, this was much worse.

The woman's body was lying chest down on a blue tarp, her head turned to the right as if she wanted to look out the window. Instead her dead eyes stared at a drawing of a Celtic cross with a single rose housed in a wooden frame. Something about it seemed familiar. *She* seemed familiar.

I could hear Molly on the phone, but she sounded far away. I bent over to get a closer look at the woman. She had platinum blonde hair draped carefully over her left shoulder. Her blue tee shirt was pulled halfway up her back and she was missing a large piece of flesh from the lower back area. I covered my mouth to control my breathing and to keep the nausea at bay from not only seeing the exposed muscle in this woman's back, but from the odor beginning to form around her. I had no clue how I'd missed the smell before. As I stood up, I caught sight of her right arm. It was bent as if she might attempt a pushup at any moment.

I stared at the woman's face.

I knew her. I'd seen her that night at Food Park.

She was the woman the creature had whispered to Monday night. The woman with the pretty tattoo on her arm. Except it wasn't on her arm anymore.

The police showed up first, then the paramedics, and then an entire parade of officers and forensics investigators. Molly and I were shooed into the hallway and questioned by Officer Vick for at least fifteen minutes. Mrs. Hiroto came over and questioned her daughter while glaring hard at me. I knew Molly's mother wouldn't make a scene in public, especially while she was working the case, but I felt Molly might be grounded for a long while and it was all my fault.

Officer Vick asked us to wait in the hall until the lead investigator showed up for questioning. Of course, where else would I go? I slid down a locker and onto the floor across from the Art Room. Various officers and other very-important-people poured in and out of the room. I could see flashes of light from the forensic team's cameras as they continued to collect evidence. They'd brought in giant lights and ran cords to illuminate the crime scene as well as the hallway.

After a short while, both Detective Graham and Detective Tudor arrived. Detective Graham frowned in my direction as he walked into the Art Room.

"Great. He's going to be the one to question us."

"Who?" Molly asked.

I nodded my head towards the Art Room. "Detective Graham. I met him the other day at the gym. He was working out. I forgot to tell you."

Molly made a sound of approval, but I shot her a look. Now was not the time to check out the detective.

Both detectives were in the room for a long time talking with the forensics team. Detective Graham spoke with Officer Vick, apparently about Molly and me as both men motioned in our direction.

When Detective Graham finally emerged from the room, he was by himself. I slowly stood. I couldn't help but notice how handsome he was tonight. He did look young, but he had an aged look behind his eyes. I suppose anyone investigating murder cases for a living had probably seen worse than the poor woman in the Art Room.

He must have been off duty because he wore a pair of jeans, long sleeve white thermal with the sleeves pushed up, and a baseball cap. His watch was on his left wrist and a few leather bracelets on his right. His side arm was still on though.

He scowled at me as Molly stood up.

"I took the liberty of calling your mother because I can't question you until she arrives," he said. His green eyes bore into mine, and I may have stopped breathing.

"However, your mother already gave me permission," he said to Molly. "I'm Detective Graham." He held out his hand and Molly shook it as she smiled up at him in her usual flirtatious manner. I suddenly felt aggravated, although I wasn't entirely sure why.

"We can speak over here." He motioned for Molly to follow him over to the far end of the hall by the classroom we hadn't investigated on this floor.

As Detective Graham questioned Molly, I peered into the Art Room again. People were milling about everywhere, but they still hadn't moved the body.

"There you are!" I jumped at the sound of my mother's voice. This was going to be bad. Mom was walking at a fast clip toward me with Ben trailing behind her, dodging quick moving officers. Although a confrontation with her was the last thing I wanted, I moved towards her as fast as I could before she could reach the entrance to the Art Room. Not to spare Mom the gruesome scene, after all she wrote horror novels, but to shield Ben from a sight he would never forget.

"Mom, stop, before you come any further. It's…she's…in the old Art Room." I put my hands up and shot her a knowing look. Ben was all eyes and ears. He was fascinated by this real crime scene.

Mom sighed loudly and grabbed my arm and pulled me down the hall and around the corner away from the scene where most of the officers couldn't see us. Ben almost tripped trying to keep up.

When we were out of view, she let go and half-whispered half-exploded. "What were you thinking, Ainsley? My God, I can't trust you to come home from school now. Why did you come in here?"

I wasn't sure what to say. I couldn't tell her about the creature that emerged from the building. What was Molly telling Detective Graham? Whatever story I told Mom right now would probably contradict Molly's story.

"I know, Mom. I'm sorry. I've always loved this building and, on a whim, today, I tried the door and it was unlocked."

"It was unlocked, so you waltzed right on in? Have you ever heard of trespassing? You could be charged."

"I thought I would come in and look around. Maybe take some pictures. I'm glad I came in though, Mom. If not, how long do you think that poor woman would've been here?"

Mom stared me down until I looked away. She had a knack of doing that. Mentally disciplining me somehow.

"Ben, stay here," Mom barked the order to my younger brother. He didn't move as she pulled me further into the corner near the double doors to the stairwell. She lowered her voice, not just so Ben wouldn't hear, but neither could the investigators around the corner. "This is serious, Ainsley. If you are lying about anything, the police will find out and it will appear as if you had something to do with this woman's death. Do you understand?" She was practically shaking me.

"Yes, Mom," I answered. I hadn't thought of it that way. I'd practically been at the first crime scene and now I'd found this body. Plus, I still hadn't told the police I recognized the woman from the grocery store. I hadn't told Mom either.

"Mrs. Reynolds?" Detective Graham had rounded the corner and now stood next to Ben.

Mom quickly regained her composure. She dropped her hands from my arms and we walked back to the waiting Detective. "Thank you for calling me, Detective Graham," she said, as she placed an arm around Ben.

"Of course. If it's all right, I'd like to ask Ainsley a few questions about today."

"Yes, let me see if Molly will keep an eye on Ben for a moment." Mom left us and turned up the hall to find Molly.

"Hi, buddy," Detective Graham smiled at Ben. "I'll have your mom and sister out of here in no time, okay?"

Ben smiled. "That's okay. It's cool, but is Ainsley in trouble?"

The detective studied me with those green eyes, and sighed. "Not if I can help it."

Before Detective Graham could say anything else, Mom came back with Molly.

"I'm going to take him outside to the field. There is plenty of light from the streetlamps and it's not quite dark, yet." Molly caught my eye as she passed with Ben. "What a day for us to decide to creep, huh?"

I nodded my head as I silently praised my best friend for what she'd told the detective. It was basically the same story I'd told Mom about wanting to investigate this place.

Detective Graham turned a page in his notebook. "Okay, Ainsley, how did you wind up here today?"

"I was walking home from school and thinking about this book that Molly and I read by David Morrell about "creepers", people who investigate abandoned buildings and search for interesting objects left behind. We'd always wanted to go on an urban exploring adventure and so I tried the front door, on a whim, and it opened."

"So, you came inside? No other reason to make you want to enter the building?"

"No. I called Molly because I'd promised Mom I wouldn't go into any buildings alone." I could practically feel Mom rolling her eyes.

Detective Graham studied me for a moment before he wrote something down in his notebook. "After the two of you came in, what happened next?"

"We investigated the first and second floors. We wandered around the library and music room, and then came up here to this floor. We went to this room first," I pointed to the old science room before continuing, "and then made our way to the Art Room. That's when we saw her. Not at first, then all at once. Suddenly, she was the only thing in the room."

"Did you hear anything when you came into the room or on this floor?"

"No, the whole building was quiet."

"Did you touch the body?"

"No, but I did get close enough to see her face and determine she was dead. I saw her wounds. Did the same person who killed the first victim kill her too?" I asked.

Detective Graham closed his notebook. "We don't know yet. It's still an ongoing investigation. We are looking into a few leads. Is there anything else you can tell me?"

I glanced nervously at Mom and then back to Detective Graham. "I think I recognize the woman."

"From where?" Mom asked, before the Detective could chime in.

"Monday night when I ran to Food Park to pick up a cake. She was shopping down Aisle Eight. I recognized the tattoo on her arm. It's of a flower wrapped around a Celtic cross. I wish I could give you more information."

"No, that's great, Ainsley. That gives me another lead. I can check with the store's security cameras to see if she was recorded. Maybe she used a debit or credit card and we can possibly identify her that way by tracing her address and confirming it with the forensics team."

Detective Graham placed his hand on my shoulder. "But you have got to promise me that you will not go into any more empty buildings. I don't care if your friend Molly is with you or your mother or an entire group of friends. You have got to let me, and the others, investigate this and solve these murders." He turned his head back to the crime scene before dropping his hand from my shoulder. 'Call me if you think of anything else."

I nodded my head as he thanked Mom. I didn't know why I felt like crying. Maybe because I'd somehow disappointed Detective Graham after he'd told me not to follow any more suspicious men into buildings. Technically, I hadn't *followed* anyone into the building, but nonetheless, the detective was not happy with my latest antic.

And that fact really bothered me.

I waved goodbye to Molly outside the junior high school building and rode home with Mom and Ben. Mom appeared tired, so I offered to throw a frozen pizza into the oven and she agreed. After Mom got Ben ready for bed, she said she was headed downstairs to her office to work on the research and outline for the next book in her series before she had to tackle the revisions for the rough draft of the other book. I decided it was best to wait until morning to ask her if I could go to Charlotte with Molly to attend Elijah's exhibit at Queens.

After a quick shower, I tossed on a sleep shirt and grabbed my backpack. I still had homework in three subjects and had wasted so much time at the school waiting on investigators. Every bit of energy I had was sapped, but if my grades dropped, Mom would finally blow a gasket.

I hated the fact that I was putting Mom through this, but what could I do. For some reason, I was the only person who could see these creatures, who Raymond referred to as the Muladach. I couldn't tell Mom about them. She'd probably chalk it up to teen angst and emotional trauma brought on by Dad's death and force me to see a psychiatrist.

And then I would wind up in the room next to Raymond Moore's in the mental health ward.

Three hours later, I finally finished all of my homework and submitted the assignments electronically to the appropriate teachers. I'd had work in Literature, Chemistry, and Calculus. Now that my brain was officially fried, I threw everything into my backpack and plugged my iPad up to the charger. I turned on the alarm and switched off the lamp.

I sighed loudly as I allowed my body to sink into the bed. I was tired, but just as I was succumbing to sleep, a thought started to nag at the back of my mind. Detective Graham planned to observe the videos from the grocery store security cameras to possibly identify the woman found tonight. What if the security camera showed me knocking over the book display and talking to the woman? I hadn't told him about that because then I would've had to admit I'd seen something that caused me to turn and run.

But what if the security camera picked up the image of the creature?

I sat upright in bed. When I'd tried to film the creatures, the image came out distorted. What if the security cameras produced better results?

How could I find out without telling Detective Graham about the creatures?

The alarm clock read 11:31. I grabbed my cell phone off the nightstand and text Molly to ask if she could talk. Molly texted back that she was super tired and going to bed. I called her.

"Hey, I know you're tired, but this will only take a minute. Since your mom is on the forensics team working the case, does she have the home addresses for the other officers in the department?"

"I don't know, Ainsley. Probably not. Why?" Molly asked, in a half-yawn, half-sigh.

"Detective Graham is going to take a look at the security cameras at Food Park tomorrow to see if he can locate the woman. I'm wondering if the footage also picked up the creature." I could barely contain my excitement. If the video showed the creature, then everyone would know they existed.

"Why do you need an address?"

"I need to let Detective Graham know I ran into that woman and there might be something unexplainable on the video. I need to tell him before he watches it."

"Ainsley, the only way you can tell him that is if you admit you saw a demon or whatever. He's going to think you're crazy. Plus, don't you have his business card? His phone number is on it. Call him in the morning."

"I think it would be better if I can gauge his reaction face-to-face."

"Hmmm, I'm sure that's why," Molly snorted. "I think you want his address because he's hot and you're clearly into him."

"What? That's not true. Does your mom have his address or not?" I was not amused with my best friend's very perceptive allegation.

"Okay. Let me check and if she does, I'll text it to you. Then I'm going to sleep."

After I hung up from Molly, I slipped out of my room and headed to the kitchen. Mom's bedroom door was open, but she wasn't in her room which meant she was still in her office working on the book. She got pretty involved during the outlining phase.

I made myself a cup of coffee and reached for a can of Dr. Pepper in the refrigerator but changed my mind at the last second and grabbed a bottle of water. I only needed a little caffeine if I had to wait for Molly.

I kept the light off in my room since I didn't want Mom to see it under the door if she went to bed soon. I scrolled through Facebook and Instagram as I waited. Thirty minutes ticked by and still no word from Molly. Maybe her mother didn't keep information like that at home. Maybe Molly had gone to bed.

As I started to feel let-down, a text came through from Molly. It read: **Alec Graham, 4310 Lanier Lane. Mom had it listed in her phone. Going to bed.**

I text back: **Thanks. I'm going over in the AM. Don't pick me up.**

Then I threw in a few emojis before hitting send. I screenshot the address and saved it to my Favorites to make sure I could easily find it in the morning.

CHAPTER FIVE

The next morning, I got up much earlier than usual, before Mom and Ben. I showered and dressed and left Mom a note letting her know I planned to meet some friends before school to go over a Literature assignment before the test. I also asked her if I could, pretty please, go with Molly to an Art Exhibit at Queens University as one of her friends was the featured artist. I also threw in the obligatory "I love you, heart" so she wouldn't worry. I hated lying to her, but this was too important to let go.

Lanier Lane wasn't far from my street. Of course, in this small town, you could drive from one end to the other in less than fifteen minutes. Lanier Lane was a quaint little street with lots of brick houses nestled neatly in a row. I preferred more space between the neighbors as these houses set pretty close to one another. I couldn't think of any of my friends who lived on this street, but there was one snobby girl named Rowan Wesley who lived near the end. I only remembered that fact because we had Girl Scouts together and her mother invited me to her birthday party. Rowan had been horrible to me although I couldn't remember why now. There probably was never a real reason. The ridiculous girl had made fun of my outfit and declared I smelled like possum pee.

Whatever.

I'd told Mom that I never wanted to go back to that girl's house again and eventually dropped out of Scouts because of Rowan. Now, I steered clear of her in school which wasn't much of a problem as we ran in different circles and I rarely ever saw her.

I slowed down as I came close to house number 4310. I recognized the black SUV parked in front as the one from my house the other day. The small brick home was nice, but there were large brick flower beds attached to the front of the house without any flowers in them or fall decorations. That was a shame.

I stepped up onto the covered front porch and noticed two blue wooden Arondack chairs and a matching table between them and wondered if Detective Graham ever sat out here and drank his coffee in the morning. Did he drink coffee?

There wasn't a doorbell, so I opened the glass door and knocked loudly on the maroon door. Through the door's frosted oval glass, I could see movement before the door opened. A petite young woman dressed in a pajama short set stood in the doorway. She appeared college-aged with her dark hair pulled up into one of those cute messy buns I could never figure out with my thick hair.

"Uh, hi. Is Detective Graham here?" I asked, completely flustered. This was not how I thought this would go. I'd actually rehearsed what I was going to say to him when he opened the door.

The woman looked me up and down. "Sure, come on in. Is he expecting you this early?"

As I stepped into the living room and started to answer her, a voice boomed through the small house. "Hey, Kels, do you think you could pick up pizza for..." Detective Graham stopped short at the doorway into the room. He held a towel around his waist, apparently fresh from a shower. I tried to stare at the carpet at my feet, but found my eyes darting back to him. I'd never seen a man look like that before as every muscle in his body was defined, right down to the V-shaped cuts disappearing behind his towel.

"Ainsley, what are you doing here?" Of course, the detective would sound shocked that I stood in his living room.

I averted my eyes again and focused on the plush brown carpet. Nice choice. This shade would go with any color of furniture. I couldn't focus with him standing there, naked, with a towel.

I needed to say something, but I mutely stared at my shoes. I'd worn my cute black ankle boots with a pair of black skinny jeans and a longer ribbed V-neck sweater. I'd made sure I'd applied a full face of makeup and wore my hair down although it was probably a little windblown by now. I had no idea why I felt the need to dress up pretty to see Detective Graham.

"Ainsley, are you all right?" he asked.

"I, there was something I needed to tell you before you view the surveillance video from Food Park." I raised my eyes to look at him. He seemed to consider my words and then he slowly walked towards me with one hand up in the air and the other holding his towel closed.

"You could have called me. Or text. That's why I gave you my number. How did you know where I live?"

I evaded the question. "I'm sorry. You're right. I wanted to catch you before you left for the store."

Detective Graham glanced back and forth from me to the woman he'd called Kels like a deer caught in the headlights of an oncoming car during hunting season.

"It's okay. Let me get dressed and I'll take you to school. You can fill me in on the way. You are going to school this morning, right?"

"Yes," I answered, as I thumbed the strap on my backpack.

"Okay, give me a few minutes." He turned to the woman, who raised an eyebrow at him. "Kelsey, this is Ainsley Reynolds. Ainsley, this is my girlfriend, Kelsey Chambers."

Of course, he has a girlfriend.

I watched him turn and hurry out of the room to get dressed. I couldn't help but stare at his back. Never mind that the muscles were so defined they appeared chiseled like the marble statue of a demigod, but a large tattoo adorned his back from the nape of his neck across his shoulders and down to his lower back. No matter how hard I strained, I couldn't make out the detail from this vantage point near the front door. I could only see the wings of something on his shoulder blades. But my, I couldn't help but blush. None of the boys in school came close to that. Not even the football players.

Kelsey motioned for me to sit on the couch. "Can I get you anything? Maybe something to drink?"

"No, thank you. I'm fine," I said as I sat down at the end of the couch to wait.

"Okay. Well, I'm going to run back into the kitchen and finish making my breakfast. I have class at eight."

"Where do you go?" I asked her.

"The Community College over in Riverston. I'm working on my LPN. Licensed Practical Nurse," she explained, when I gave her a blank look. "You're in high school, I take it?"

"Yes, I'm a senior this year."

"I went to Riverston High where I grew up. I actually thought you were older when I first saw you. I thought maybe you worked with Alec.

Well, I'd better get going. If you need me, I'll be in the kitchen." Kelsey bounded out of the living room in her Ugg-like houseboots.

I glanced around the detective's living room. It had a nice brick fireplace and a large wooden coffee table. The couch matched the carpet and appeared to recline. Across the room was a large television mounted on the wall with two different game consoles on a table underneath. I leaned over the arm of the couch and snuck a peek at the bedroom to the right of the front door. All I could see was a bed with a white headboard. The bed was neatly made with a quilt on top. It was probably a guest room or something unless Detective Graham was getting dressed in the bathroom somewhere else in the house.

In my opinion, it didn't look like Kelsey lived here. Or, any woman for that matter. I couldn't detect a female touch anywhere in this room. Maybe Kelsey just spent nights?

My stomach turned a little at that thought, but I wasn't sure why. That was his business. Yes, he was handsome and probably only five years older than me. But, he was an authority figure trying to solve a murder and I was a seventeen-year-old girl who showed up at his house on a Friday morning.

I heard voices from somewhere near the back of the house and assumed it was the detective and Kelsey talking, although I couldn't make out the words. I probably didn't want to hear what they were saying anyway.

Detective Graham emerged from the next room dressed in his customary gray dress pants, dress shirt, and necktie, carrying his suit jacket. For the first time, I could see his revolver and holster up close that was hidden before by the jacket. It was different than the side arm he wore last night while in plainclothes. I wondered if this one was government issued while the other was his personal gun.

I stood up. "Detective Graham, I really am sorry to intrude," I hurriedly apologized. He stopped in front of me and gave me a tired smile.

"Alec. You can call me Alec when I'm off duty. Not that I expect you to show up at my house again, right?" he asked, raising his eyebrows at me.

"Of course not," I swore as I gave him the two raised-fingers Cub Scout sign. "I'll call first."

He laughed and shook his head. "You're starting to drive me crazy," he said, with a smile.

As we headed out the door, Kelsey called from the doorway. "It was nice to meet you, Ainsley."

Alec shut the door.

~ ~ ~

We walked to the SUV and Alec opened the passenger door for me to climb inside. It had that new car smell like Mom's car. I loved it and couldn't help but smile.

Alec saw me smiling like a dork and shook his head as he chuckled. He probably thought I was ridiculous. He waited for a car to slowly pass us before he pulled out onto the street. "Okay, so what is it you want to tell me about the video at the grocery store?"

"It's going to sound insane, but I need you to hear me out. Monday night when I went to the grocery store for Mom's cake, I walked past Aisle Eight and saw the blonde woman staring at some products on the shelves."

"The woman from the crime scene last night. She stood out to you? Why?"

I exhaled loudly. I couldn't chicken out. Not now. I had to tell him.

"It's what I saw standing beside her that made her stand out."

Alec glanced at me.

"There was a creature whispering in her ear."

Alec pulled the SUV over.

We were only a few blocks from the high school. He turned off the engine and unbuckled his seatbelt, so he could turn completely sideways in his seat to face me. "This isn't a joke. That woman is dead. Explain yourself."

"There was a creature, like a demon or something, whispering in the woman's ear. When it saw me and knew I'd seen it, then it charged straight at me. I tried to get away from it, but I fell over a display of books. The woman and an employee came running to my aid, but neither saw anything. The woman denied hearing or seeing anything. That's when I noticed the tattoo on her arm. The one that is now in a wooden frame."

I paused, but Alec didn't speak. He studied my face instead.

"I thought maybe the surveillance video at the store might show evidence of what I saw. I can't seem to capture the creatures on my phone. The images are distorted."

"What did you see in the elementary school parking lot?"

"A tall man…with two of the creatures."

"And yesterday?"

"I was walking home when I saw one of the creatures run out of the old building. It disappeared behind the houses across the street. I called Molly because I wanted to find out why it was in that building."

Alec was quiet for a long time. So long, that it felt like an eternity.

I continued. "I know you probably don't believe me, and I should have told you everything from the beginning, but it does sound insane. But when you watch the store video, would you check to see if there is anything strange in Aisle Eight during that time?"

Alec didn't answer me. He was deep in thought and still searching my face. Probably seriously considering committing me to a psychiatric hospital.

I reached for my backpack and withdrew the printed copy of Elijah's painting. "Here. This is what the creatures look like. The artist drew it based on the description of a demon his brother swears he saw one day on a train."

Alec slowly took the picture and studied it. I didn't say anything else. Apparently, he needed time to process my confession. Or, call for backup to contain me.

All I could do was wait. I watched as students walked on the sidewalk across the street from us towards the high school. No one bothered to look in our direction and I was thankful. If the cops did haul me away, I certainly didn't want it on YouTube.

Finally, Alec spoke. "This is the creature you saw? A demon?"

"Yes. Well, I don't know if it's a demon or not. That's what Elijah's brother called it. He calls them the Muladach because he says they drive people to madness and sorrow."

"And Molly has seen this, too?"

"No, but she believes me."

"So, you're the only one to have seen it?"

"And the artist's brother."

"Where is he?"

"In the mental health ward at the hospital in Charlotte."

Alec raised his brows at me again. "So, only you and a mental patient have seen this creature?"

I fought the urge to roll my eyes. "I know what it sounds like, but I'm telling you the truth."

Alec flipped the paper over and withdrew a pen from his shirt pocket. "What's the artist's name again and his brother's name?"

I gave Alec Elijah's and Raymond's names and info as best I could. He kept his face neutral, so I couldn't tell if he believed me or not.

"I'm going to keep this, all right?" he said, holding up the picture. I nodded my head as he put his seatbelt back on and started the engine. "I'm going to drop you off at school, and then get Detective Tudor before heading to the store. Do you have your cell on you?"

"Yes, of course."

"After I view the surveillance footage, I'll text you and let you know if I saw anything...odd."

He pulled the SUV up in front of the school as the drop off line was clear. I was later than I'd expected. Classes would start soon.

I got out and walked around the front of the truck, stopping at his window. I smiled as he lowered it. "Thank you for checking it out. I was afraid you'd think I was crazy."

Alec didn't smile back this time. Instead he looked genuinely concerned. "Just be careful and don't go anywhere alone."

~ ~ ~

I met up with Molly in the cafeteria, but it was too late to grab a bite to eat. Our other friends had already left for class when I realized I hadn't eaten since last night. I would have to eat lunch.

"Hey, how'd it go?" Molly asked.

"Well, I don't think he thinks I'm crazy. I told him everything and he listened. I think if he thought I was insane, he would have argued with me or something."

"What's he going to do?" Molly asked, popping the last bite of bagel in her mouth.

"He promised he would look for anything strange in the footage from the store. He'll let me know what they find. Hopefully, something will show up. I also had to give him Elijah and Raymond's names because of the painting."

Molly stood up to empty her tray. "I'll text Elijah and let him know. You didn't tell him how you knew where he lived, did you?"

"No, I would never do that. Are we still going to the exhibit this evening?"

"Oh yeah, I've already picked out an outfit to make Elijah blush."

I laughed. I hadn't thought about what to wear to this thing tonight. Plus, I still needed to make sure it was approved through Mom. As we moved down the hall talking about Elijah and the art show tonight, I practically ran into Rowan Wesley and a couple of her friends.

I muttered an apology and tried to move past, but Rowan blocked my path. I made eye contact with Medusa's spawn, her red hair perfectly coiffed. I'd just thought about the horribly snobby Rowan this morning. Apparently, I'd telepathically summoned her.

Rowan ran her hand over her sideways bangs. "So, I saw you this morning."

"What?" I asked. Molly moved in closer. Most people didn't mess with Molly. She was small, but fierce, loud, and a fighter. Rowan didn't seem aware of Molly's presence though.

"I saw you on my street this morning on my way to school. You were coming out of that cop's house. He's a detective, right? No wonder you've been dressing better." She narrowed her eyes as she took in my outfit. "Got yourself a little glow going on, but isn't he a little old to be sleeping with a senior?"

Before I could respond, Molly was up in Rowan's face with a tirade of expletives. Rowan took a few steps backwards and her henchman girls started yelling at Molly but didn't dare make a move.

Mr. Clendenin, the Vice-Principal, came out of his office from hearing the commotion and stepped between Molly and Rowan. "Break it up now!" he yelled.

Molly spoke up first. "Rowan started it, Mr. Clendenin. She called Ainsley a slut."

Mr. Clendenin glared at both Molly and Rowan. "Go to class and stay away from each other the rest of the day. If I have any problems with any of you, I'll have your parents on the phone before you can utter another word."

I tugged on Molly's arm and we went around Rowan and her lackeys and right into Derek.

"So, is that true, Ains? You sleepin' with a cop?"

"Shut up, Derek," Molly said hatefully.

The boy laughed. "I knew there was something different about you," he yelled back, as he went on his way to class.

"I hate her," Molly growled through gritted teeth. "She's always been like that."

"Don't I know it. Thanks for jumping in and defending me. I was in shock that she saw me at Alec's, I mean, Detective Graham's house."

Molly stopped in front of her first period class. "You called him Alec. Are you two on a first name basis now?"

"Ha ha," I said, rolling my eyes. "He said I could call him that when he's off duty. I don't think he was too thrilled I showed up there this morning. Anyways, he has a girlfriend. I met her."

"Oh, really?" Molly shot me an odd look.

"Yes," I I jokingly shoved Molly backwards. "She's a college student at Riverston Community working on her LPN. She seems nice."

I had a sudden thought that landed like a sick thud in the pit of my stomach. "You don't think Rowan is going to spread rumors about me and Detective Graham, do you?"

Molly shrugged as she glanced at her watch. "I wouldn't worry about it. Most people aren't going to believe you're having an affair with a detective because that's not you. Even Derek thought it was funny. As for Rowan, she'd better not or I'll personally knock her teeth down her throat and use her hair for extensions." With that, Molly walked into her classroom and left me standing in the hall as the tardy bell rang.

~ ~ ~

By lunchtime, I felt anxious. Alec hadn't text yet, and I wondered if he did think I'd lost my mind. Maybe he'd driven to my house and told Mom. Mom would kill me just for showing up at the detective's house, let alone for thinking I hallucinated demons.

Demons. The Muladach.

That's what Raymond called them, and I wondered if that's what they truly were. They were grotesque and exactly how I would imagine a real demon to appear. As my friends ate all around me at our table in the cafeteria, I pulled my phone out of my back pocket. I searched the town library's website and found several e-books about demons. I downloaded every one of them as it was much easier than walking to the library after school.

"So, what's his name?" Derek leaned over as if trying to sneak a peek at my phone. I moved it away from him as the e-book "Demons of Lore" opened.

"Derek, leave her alone." Bronwyn nestled into Derek's side, but he continued to stare at me. "If Ainsley is finally dating again, then I say let it go." She rolled her big brown eyes over to me. "If he's the one I've seen around town, then I say you do you, girl."

Derek frowned at his girlfriend and then turned back to me as if waiting for an answer. "I'm only saying you've been looking pretty hot lately for *some*body."

Bronwyn punched him in the arm.

"For *myself*. Rowan is full of crap and you know it. Don't believe her lies," I answered back. Before I could defend myself some more, my phone vibrated, and I glanced down. A message from Alec dropped down and I clicked on it to fully open it.

It read: **There's something on the video. I need you to watch it. I'll call your mother for permission.**

I text back **OK** and then slid my phone back into my pocket. I'd have to tell Molly, so she wouldn't wait for me after school.

Everyone had gone back to eating except Derek. He stared at me as if seeing me for the first time. I finally got up and dumped my full tray of food into the trash and went out into the hallway to wait until the end of lunch.

~ ~ ~

During fifth period, I received another text from Alec informing me that he and Detective Tudor would pick me up after school to view the video at the police station. For some reason, I was a little bummed that Detective Tudor would be with him.

The rest of the afternoon, my mind kept reverting back to seeing Alec wrapped in that towel and Rowan's accusations of me sleeping with the detective. Part of me was scared to death a rumor like that would get started. News like that would cause Alec to lose his job on the force, or worse. Of course, the accusations weren't true, but I guessed Alec hadn't told anyone that I'd been to his house today either. Obviously, he hadn't told Mom, or I would've heard about it by now.

The other part of me, the secret part, was excited over the mere thought of catching the eye of Detective Alec Graham. But, I couldn't tell that to anyone, not even Molly.

I noticed several boys in my afternoon classes looking me up and down or smiling at me if we made eye contact. That normally didn't happen, especially since I'd gained twenty pounds. I usually tried to hide the gain with my billowy tunics. Rowan was right about that. I was dressing better. I was back to wearing form-fitting clothes again, but that still didn't explain the boys' reactions to my new curves. Was it because of Rowan's accusation? Did these guys think that if I put out for an older man, like Alec, I would probably put out for them too? It would explain why suddenly Derek kept giving me the all-smiles.

I couldn't wait for the end of the school day.

~ ~ ~

Alec's black SUV was waiting for me when I walked out of the school building. He leaned against the back-passenger door and opened it for me as I got closer. He smiled and gave me that little wink. Did he do that to everyone? I would like to think it was only for me.

"Learn anything new?" he asked in a low voice, as I slid onto the backseat.

"Calculus is the devil," I answered.

"Amen." He smiled and shut the door.

I spoke a quick hello to Detective Tudor who sat in the front passenger seat, frowning.

"Wait!" I heard Molly's voice as she ran to the truck. She said a hi to the detectives and then stuck her head in Alec's open door. "Don't forget about the show tonight. I'll call you before I leave."

"Okay, thanks, Mol," I said, and waved at her. She waved back and started her walk towards the school parking lot.

When Alec shut his door, I pulled my seatbelt on and noticed Rowan Wesley watching me from the front steps of the school. I pretended I didn't see her. For crying out loud, if I was sleeping with the detective, then wouldn't I be sitting up front? And why on earth would we flaunt a relationship in front of his partner? Stupid, jealous girl.

Alec pulled away from the curb and peered at me through the rearview mirror. "What show are you going to?"

"What?" I asked, caught off guard by his question.

"Molly is going to pick you up for a show?" he asked, glancing back and forth between my reflection and the road.

"The artist, Elijah Moore, who painted that picture I gave you, is featured at an Art Exhibit tonight at Queens University in Charlotte. He invited Molly to attend, but she won't go without me."

Alec frowned. "With everything that's happened the last few days, maybe traveling out of town isn't such a good idea, especially to hang out with a guy you just met this week."

Detective Tudor shot Alec a look of warning. I wasn't sure what that meant. Detectives were hard to figure out.

I smiled at Alec's green eyes in the mirror. "Well, I met Elijah on Wednesday, the same day I met the two of you, and yet, here I am. Hanging out. Plus, I have to go. I promised Molly." Neither detective said anything else for the remainder of the drive to the police station.

~ ~ ~

When we arrived at the police station, the detectives led me to a small room to view the confiscated video.

"I filled Detective Tudor in with what you claim you saw at the grocery store and again at the schools. I showed him the picture you gave me when I ran into you this morning on my way to work," Alec shot me a look as he scooted a metal chair over to me.

Of course, he'd told his partner about the creature. They were both investigating the same case. However, I noticed he'd changed the facts about how he came across the painting. He'd left out the minute detail that I'd been to his house this morning. I glanced up at Detective Tudor's skeptical face.

Alec continued, "I questioned the store clerk from that night, but you were right. He didn't see anything."

A man came into the room and Detective Tudor introduced him as the video tech. The man sat down in front of the equipment and after a few seconds, the surveillance video popped up on one of the monitors. It was in black and white and covered different areas of the store in little frames.

Another monitor came to life as the video tech switched back and forth between the different cameras.

After a moment, the video tech slowed the footage down and I saw myself walk to the automatic doors at Food Park and then stop to talk to the young mother and her little girl.

"Do you know them?" Detective Tudor asked, as he took a chair next to mine.

"No. I passed them on my way in and the little girl dropped her sucker. I gave her a children's book to stop her from crying."

Alec shed his suit jacket and then leaned down behind me as he watched the video. "That was sweet."

I could smell his body wash from this morning and I narrowed my eyes to focus harder on the video as the technician switched between cameras to follow my every move. The video showed me picking out the cake for Mom and spending a little too much time admiring the baked goods.

Suddenly, video-Ainsley froze and glanced around with confusion etched on her face.

"Wait," I said, and the tech paused the video. "I felt someone watching me while I was standing there, but no one was around."

The tech switched between all the cameras. Sure enough, not one customer or employee was anywhere near the bakery area. Both detectives nodded their heads as the tech resumed the footage.

Video-Ainsley walked through the store and held the cake in front of her like a $4.99 treasure. She paused briefly at the pepperoni rolls. I rolled my eyes. Did the videos have to show everything?

As she passed Aisle Eight, she stopped. Then took a few steps backwards.

"There," I practically yelled. The video paused again. "I'd heard an animal snarling and thought maybe a stray had got into the store somehow, but as I passed this aisle I saw something else. There's the woman."

The tech zoomed in. The woman with the platinum blonde hair stood like a statue in front of the shelves, as I remembered her. The tech zoomed out again to show video-Ainsley motionless at the front of the aisle. Suddenly, a black mist formed behind the woman.

"There! There it is," I exclaimed, as I jumped up and almost knocked the chair over. I stared at the detectives as I pointed at the screen.

The tech zoomed in slowly. It wasn't the full-fledged demon I'd seen that night, but the cameras did pick up something. He played the video. The mist took on the shape of a dense black mass behind the woman. The video zoomed out again as the mass darted straight for video-Ainsley who turned and ran smack into the turn-style of books. The plastic container of cake bounced like a ball away from her. I moved in for a closer look. As she was on all fours trying to climb out from under the heavy weight of the books, the mass hovered above her for a moment, almost like a shadow figure, and then disappeared. The video showed the employee running to her aid, and then the woman.

I sat back down in the chair in shock. The footage had caught something, although it wasn't exactly what I'd seen, it was something not of this world.

The technician reversed the feed and pointed at the black mass as he addressed the detectives. "As I stated before I can't say exactly what the anomaly is, but it's not her shadow or the shadow of the woman walking down the aisle to check on her after she fell."

Detective Tudor nodded his head. "You mentioned it before, but I want to clarify, that the black spot on the footage is not due to a defect in the surveillance equipment?"

The technician shook his head emphatically. "Absolutely not. *That* I can tell you. If it was, it would be elsewhere on the footage, but I've studied every bit of this video for that entire day. This is the only moment that it shows up and it's only on the film for exactly eighteen seconds." Detective Tudor thanked the technician as he walked him to the doorway of the room.

Eighteen seconds. Sounded like a small amount of time, but it had lasted forever. I was so caught up in what I'd seen on the video that I didn't hear Alec turn the chair next to mine.

"Hey, are you all right?" he asked quietly.

I peered at him through tears that threatened to spill down my face any moment. He straddled the chair and folded his arms over the back.

I nodded my head.

"You look like you might cry," he whispered.

I nodded again. "You detectives and your observation skills," I whispered and smiled. "It's the fact that something shows up in the video. Something that proves what I've been seeing is real. What Raymond Moore saw is real. It appeared as a black shadow on there, but I saw it for what it truly is. I didn't hallucinate it. There's nothing wrong with me."

He studied me for a moment as the tears began to stream down my face. I let them fall, but I refused to turn this into an ugly cry. He placed his hand on my shoulder.

"We'll figure this out. I promise," he whispered back.

I nodded my head again as I wiped the tears with the sleeve of my sweater. "It's still out there. And there's more than one."

"Detective Graham?" Detective Tudor stood in the doorway with an officer. His eyes darted from me to Alec's hand on my shoulder and finally landed on the detective. Alec let his hand drop as he stood up from the chair.

"What's wrong?"

"There's been another murder."

~ ~ ~

Another police officer drove me home in a squad car. I'd had to wait an hour at the station because of the chaos that ensued after Detective Tudor announced there had been another murder. He and Alec had left quickly with a slew of officers. Alec had given this officer the order to drive me home safely, but I'd had to wait until he was free. I thanked him as Mom opened the front door.

She held the screen door open. "Everything okay? The detectives said they needed you to identify the blonde woman from last night in the Food Park security videos."

I nodded as I walked up the stairs to the living room and dropped my backpack on the couch. "Yeah, it's fine. That was her in the store that night."

Mom sank down onto the love seat. "That's horrible. She must have been taken not long afterwards."

I didn't answer, but instead went into the kitchen for a bottle of water. I downed half of it before I rejoined her in the living room. I couldn't believe how thirsty I was.

"Mom, I never did hear back from you about tonight's Art Exhibit. I promised Molly I would go, and she won't go alone."

Mom made a face. "I don't know, Ainsley. I really don't like the idea of you two girls going that far with two murders recently in town."

"But, we won't be in town. We'll be in Charlotte. Molly is really looking forward to going. She's already picked out her outfit and everything. She's considering Queens for college." Of course, Mom didn't know about the third murder yet. But Molly had been a great friend this week, going above and beyond, when I needed support. She'd been willing to search an abandoned building with me as well as search her mother's phone for Alec's address.

I couldn't tell Mom any of that.

Mom stood up with worry etched across her face and I followed her into the kitchen. I grabbed another bottle of water out of the refrigerator. I'd already finished my first one. Mom reached for my bottle and I handed it to her, so I pulled a second one out for myself.

"Maybe if there were someone else going with you two girls. What about Molly's parents?"

"They both have to work this evening. Mrs. Hiroto is up to her eyeballs in this case and I think Dr. Hiroto is out of town. There will be other people there. It's at a university."

"I know. I feel uneasy about the trip back," she admitted, as she stared out the kitchen window.

I leaned on the counter next to her. She was scared for us. I was about to give up and call Molly when the doorbell rang. I followed Mom to the top of the stairs as she went to the front door.

Alec stood at the door, sans Detective Tudor. "Mrs. Reynolds, I'm sorry to bother you again today, but would it be possible to speak to Ainsley for a moment?"

"Of course, you can, Detective Graham. Anything we can do to help catch this murderer." Mom moved to the side and allowed Alec to slide by her. I backed away from the top step as he ascended the stairs. It had only been a couple of hours since I'd seen him, but his face wore a weary expression. Was this crime scene as awful as the one at the junior high?

I moved my backpack, so he could sit down on the couch, then I sat on the opposite end. Why did this feel weird with Mom in the room? A few hours ago, he'd been so close I could detect the woodsy scent of his body wash. Now, I didn't want Mom to see me that close to him.

"Ainsley, can I ask you a few questions? It's about the newest victim."

"Newest victim?" Mom asked, and I winced. There went my plans with Molly.

"We found a third body this afternoon at the old train station depot near the river," he said. I could see dark circles beginning to form under his eyes.

Mom shook her head. "This is why I decided you shouldn't go tonight."

"Go where?" Alec asked, as he glanced in my direction.

"The Art Exhibit at Queens University in Charlotte. Molly invited me, and she won't go alone. I told you about it earlier."

Alec was quiet for a moment. "It's probably better if the two of you stick together actually. Molly shouldn't go alone," he said before turning to Mom. "It would probably be safer for Ainsley to go with her friend than for her friend to go by herself honestly."

Mom frowned as she sat down on the love seat. "But what about the murders, Detective Graham?"

"I know, but they've been local to here. We haven't learned of any related murders in Charlotte. We do know that the murderer, or murderers, take the victims while they're alone."

I watched as Mom studied Alec, and then finally nodded her head at me. "I'll have to think about it."

"If it would make you feel any better, I could make sure the girls have a police escort to and from the show."

"You can do that?" I asked. With all the police manpower placed on the investigation, I couldn't believe the department would send an escort with me.

"Seems strange the police department would do that with a serious investigation underway," Mom said, apparently, she was thinking the same thing. Of course, she would. Mom wrote books and spent time with the police to make sure her facts were straight.

Alec didn't bat an eyelash. "I can personally take them and bring them back. Other than questioning Ainsley about the third victim, we're calling it early tonight to start fresh tomorrow while the M.E. does their part with the autopsy." He met my gaze. "She's our primary material witness in this case. My job is to keep her safe."

I could see the struggle in Mom's eyes to make the right decision. Finally, she relented. "You can go, but only if he takes you girls, and you stay in his sight."

I smiled. I would do my best.

CHAPTER SIX

Alec stayed a few minutes longer while he asked if I knew of a man named Rupert Means from South Carolina or if I'd seen anything unusual. It was hard to answer him with Mom sitting so close. She didn't know about the creatures or the black shape on the surveillance videos. I told him I didn't recognize that name.

At the front door, Alec agreed to pick me up at seven o'clock, and then we'd collect Molly. After he left, I thanked Mom and ran to my room to choose an outfit and call Molly to let her know about the change in plans.

Molly had mentioned she'd taken extra time to choose an outfit to impress Elijah tonight. I needed to find something equally important. It wasn't so much that I wanted to impress Alec, but I suddenly wanted him to look at me differently. Kind of like the boys did today in school - with the exception that Alec treated me with respect, and in my book, that was huge.

The problem was he probably viewed me as his seventeen-year-old high-school-senior material witness in a case. And, technically, I was. Well, I wasn't sure what material I could present in a trial, but I was still a witness to something.

I stood in front of my closet surveying everything. Suddenly, I knew I wanted to dress as an intelligent and classy young woman. How a woman his age would dress. Apparently, smart women were his forte – like Kelsey Chambers.

The thought of Kelsey made me stop in my tracks. What was I doing? Alec had a girlfriend. Clearly one who spent nights with him and made breakfast and picked up pizza when he didn't have time. He was probably home right now telling her about having to take two girls to an exhibit in Charlotte, so he could keep them safe because it was his job. Like he told Mom.

Maybe he would bring Kelsey along for date night.

I was the witness in his investigation. I needed to remember that.

~ ~ ~

I cleared my mind of all thoughts about Alec and Kelsey while I got dressed. I took my time with my hair and makeup to get that classy, yet sultry look. I flat ironed my long hair, and then curled wide ringlets about one-third of the way from the ends. Hopefully, the curls would last the evening. I chose a heather gray sheath dress that hit right above my knee with a pair of black calf-high boots with heels. I added a black and gray scarf around my neck and pinned it with a rhinestone broach in the shape of a skeleton key.

I stared at my reflection in the floor-length mirror behind my bedroom door. Classy with curves.

I had just switched bags to a black clutch when Mom called down the hall that Detective Graham was at the door.

I glanced at my reflection one more time in the mirror on my dresser, but this time my eyes landed on the image of Dad's picture on my desk.

"I wish you could see me now," I whispered to the picture, before I opened the bedroom door. Picture-Dad continued to smile.

Alec stood in the living room. He was dressed in a pair of jeans with an untucked dress shirt and a black leather jacket, his hands in his pockets. I had a feeling his sidearm was under that jacket. He looked refreshed, as if he'd gone home and taken a quick nap before he showered.

This last thought brought up the fresh-from-the-shower image of Alec from this morning and I smiled all over myself like an idiot.

I caught Alec's gaze as his eyes flitted over my outfit. He grinned.

There. That was the look out of his eyes I'd wanted to see, but as quickly as it appeared, it was gone again. I silently chided myself for feeling this way towards him. He had a girlfriend, and if given the choice, he would probably not want to be on a date with an almost eighteen-year-old. But this really wasn't a date. He was escorting two girls to an event. That was all.

"You look lovely. Are you ready to go?" His voice interrupted my thoughts.

"Yes, Molly is waiting on us." I held up my phone to indicate I'd already text her.

Mom walked to the front door with us but stopped Alec before he could slip out. "Remember what we talked about, Detective Graham."

"Of course, Mrs. Reynolds. You have nothing to worry about."

I followed him to the SUV and waited until he opened the front passenger door. I waved at Mom before I climbed in. I couldn't think of any high school boys I knew that held the door open for a lady. I didn't say anything other than a thank you until he started the truck and pulled away from the curb.

"What was that about?"

"What?" Alec asked, as he kept his eyes on the road.

"Mom ordered you to remember what you two talked about. What was it?"

"Oh, to keep an eye out for you and Molly, especially at the university tonight." He gave me a sideways glance. "She also reminded me that you're a senior in *high school*." He said it with a slight smile on his face.

A wave of heat filled my cheeks. "I'll be eighteen in less than two months," I uttered softly.

Alec's smile widened. "I know."

He sounded like he might laugh.

I was quiet the rest of the way to Molly's house, only piping up to give him directions. Knowing that he might view me as a schoolgirl was inevitable, but it still hurt.

I'd started to crush on him.

And he certainly didn't feel the same way.

Alec escorted Molly from her front door to the truck and held the door open for her as she slid into the backseat. Molly talked nonstop to Alec on the way to Charlotte. She asked about subjects I had no idea she was into like guns, knives, gangs, unsolved crimes, and prison.

Molly was tough at times, but not violent, so I wasn't sure if she was asking to keep the conversation up with the detective or if she was indeed considering a life of crime.

I, on the other hand, didn't speak much at all the entire trip, although Alec would look at me every so often during the drive. I was embarrassed by Mom's veiled warning to the detective and, worse, his reaction. Alec wasn't aware of my attraction to him, but his reaction to Mom's insinuation was hurtful nonetheless. If he knew what Rowan had accused us of, he'd assign Detective Tudor to safeguard me.

When we arrived on campus, Molly read the directions from Elijah to the Theatre and Arts building. Alec parked in the massive parking lot but told us to wait. He got out and surveyed the area before slowly opening our doors. He was dressed as if he didn't have a care in the world, but I knew he was on guard.

Molly looped her arm in mine and pulled me towards the building. She'd text Elijah when we arrived, but finding the event in the massive building was easy as people were strewn about the place admiring pieces of art. As we entered the first exhibit room, Elijah greeted us.

"There you are," Elijah exclaimed, as he pulled Molly into a hug. He wore a pair of jeans, untucked plaid shirt, and Converse. All of which he pulled off nicely. He couldn't seem to pull his eyes away from Molly. Her mission was accomplished with her little black dress with the asymmetrical shoulder line.

Alec cleared his throat and Elijah tore his gaze from my best friend and reached for me as he gave me a hug next. He kept his arm around my waist as I introduced him to the detective.

"Yes, we spoke on the phone about my painting. I'm glad you could make it, Detective. Actually, the original piece of that work is in Exhibit Room Number Four."

"Wow, how many exhibit rooms do you have tonight?" Molly asked him, clearly impressed.

Elijah smiled. "There are five total rooms, but my individual work is featured in Room Number Four. I have a few pieces I created with another artist in Room Number Three. Come on, I'll show you." He took Molly by the arm and reached for me with his other hand. Before I could take it, Alec interrupted.

"Why don't you two go ahead and we'll catch up with you in a few. I want to take a look at these first," Alec said, as he placed his hand on my arm.

Elijah shrugged and pulled Molly through the room. She looked back at me with a poop-eating grin that I decided to ignore. I turned to Alec and gave him a questioning look.

He glanced around at the event-goers and then touched my upper arm lightly as he guided us over to a corner of the room. "Did I say something to upset you on the drive here?"

I felt the heat rush back into my cheeks. "What do you mean?"

He still had his hand on my arm and took a step closer. I could smell his woodsy body wash again. My heart began to pound.

He lowered his voice again. "When I told you about your mother's concerns, you got quiet. My job is to protect you while you are here. You and Molly, but specifically, you. I didn't mean anything by it when I brought up the fact that you're in high school. I know you're almost eighteen. Honestly, the first time I saw you at the gym, I thought you were in your early twenties."

I allowed myself to smile at him. "That's okay, Alec. Don't worry about it. I know you're only doing your job because I'm a witness. I get it. Let's look at these pieces of art and try to have some fun." I took a step away from him. Being that close for a moment made me feel warm and fuzzy and almost dizzy.

Alec opened his mouth like he wanted to say more but instead followed me to the closest display.

"Okay, since you're here to watch over me, let me ask you a couple of questions," I said, in front of a beautiful statue of an angel. The angel stood about three feet taller than me with its hands covering its face as if it were crying. Alec studied me for a moment, and then rested his hand on the angel.

"All right, I'll play. Ask away."

"I heard you transferred from Wilmington. Is that true?"

"Yes."

"Why?"

Alec narrowed his eyes at the statue. "I'd settled in Wilmington after I served in the Marines and got out of a long relationship while I made my way up the ladder. Some things happened, and I decided I wanted to live in a smaller town. I heard from some other officers that there was an opening for a detective in Locklyn, so I applied."

He turned towards the next piece of art – a collection of beautiful blue vases hand blown by local artists into different shapes. "My commendations and solved cases got me the position pretty quickly."

"What things happened in Wilmington?"

"Nothing worth mentioning. Everyone has their fair share of demons."

"You mentioned you got out of a long relationship, so dating Kelsey is new?" I asked, as I ran my finger over the placard for the glass collection. I could feel my face burning as Alec leaned down to admire the vase in front of me.

"I guess you could call it new. Less than two months. We were set up on a blind date by a mutual friend."

I decided to change the subject quickly. "Do you think you'll catch this guy?"

Alec moved to the next art display – a bizarre painting of a man, yet his face appeared as melted wax, impossible to make out any detailed features. "I hope so before he, and those whatever they are, take another life. We believe he is working with an accomplice, someone who helps him move the bodies." He frowned at the painting. "I think with your help and ability to see these things, we may be able to track the murderer down. Believe it or not, I actually do think you are seeing *something* I can't explain."

Suddenly, he turned towards me. "My turn."

"What?"

"You asked questions. Now it's my turn to ask you questions."

"You've asked me dozens of questions every day since I met you," I laughed.

He stepped closer as we admired a wall hanging of a Native American settlement. "Those were questions for the case and they don't count."

"Oh? Okay. I'll play. Ask away."

"Are you currently dating anyone?"

"If I were, don't you think he would be here instead of you?" I watched as Alec pretended to wince from my callous remark. "Short answer, no. I haven't dated anyone in the last two years."

"Why not?"

"My dad died kind of suddenly two years ago. There was an accident and he was in a coma for a few days before it was decided that he was brain dead. We buried him less than a week later. To get through it I made my entire world revolve around Mom and Ben, school and assignments. I tuned everything else out." I smiled up at Alec. "Plus, I haven't met a boy I liked well enough to date. Or, that liked me," I laughed at my self-deprecating humor, although sadly, it was true. Up until Rowan's accusation anyway.

"I'm sorry about your father. Although, it's hard for me to believe that no one has asked you out."

"I might be a little picky. My dad told me once that just because someone wants me doesn't mean they value me. It's become my philosophy."

"It's your compass," Alec said. "It's what makes you different than some other *women*."

We walked through the remainder of Room Number One and then on to Room Number Two. We talked about the pieces of art, but my mind kept reverting back to what he thought about me being different than other women. Different in a good way. And he'd stressed *women*. He hadn't used the word *girls*.

As we entered Room Number Three, the air changed. It felt electric as if the very molecules were buzzing around me. The way it felt at the old junior high school building before we'd found the blonde woman's body. As if I'd passed through an invisible barrier.

I was light-headed. Was I hungry? When had I eaten last? I couldn't remember, but I couldn't think of anything from today.

I must've wobbled because Alec grabbed my elbow. "Woah, are you okay? You look kind of shaky."

"Yeah, I think I need to sit down. I feel light-headed. Do you find it hard to breathe in here?"

Alec shook his head as he led me over to a few chairs near the wall. "When was the last time you've eaten anything?"

I shook my head. "I'm not sure. Maybe last night."

Alec frowned. "Last night? What are you doing? Sounds like your blood sugar has dropped too low. I'm going to find you a snack and something to drink. Stay here." He squeezed my shoulder lightly and then quickly left the exhibit room.

I'd seen other guests with hors d'oeuvres throughout the building, so he was probably searching for the table. I leaned in the wing-back chair with its plush red fabric and observed the art closest to me. These pieces were beautiful. They were Celtic designs painted or stitched onto a canvas and framed. The frames themselves were ornate and seemed to go with each piece of art. I stood up to get a closer look.

I immediately swayed. I felt a strong arm move around my waist and catch me before I could fall. Everything was going black. A deep voice spoke quietly in my ear in a British accent.

"It's all right, Love. I've got you now."

~ ~ ~

When I opened my eyes, I was in the winged-back chair again with a man I didn't recognize kneeling by my side.

"There, there. Are you feeling a bit better? You fainted," he said. I hadn't imagined a British man's voice. It belonged to this man.

"Yes, I think I'm better now. My friend left to find me something to drink." A few other guests stopped by the chair to check on me while others milled around and gawked.

The man nodded his head. He was nice-looking with dark hair and dark eyes, probably a student. His eyes were such a dark brown that they almost blended in with his pupils, making them appear almost black.

I sat mesmerized by his eyes, and his accent, as he continued to talk to me. What was he saying? I needed some food. I couldn't comprehend his words.

"Ainsley? What happened?" Although Alec asked me the question, he stood over the man as if ready to pounce on him. If he hadn't said my name, I would've thought Alec was talking to him.

With shaky fingers, I reached for the cup gripped tightly in his hand. "I fainted. This man caught me before I completely embarrassed myself." I took a sip from the tiny Styrofoam cup. The sweetness from the fruit punch made me want to vomit. I forced myself to breathe deeply. I absolutely could not puke in front of both of these men.

Alec handed me a small plate with crackers and cheese cubes. "Eat this. It will help," he ordered, as he stared the cold look of death at the man.

The man slowly stood and at full height was probably four inches taller than Alec. He obviously worked out as I could see the muscles bulging from under his fitted shirt. He extended his hand out to the detective slash bodyguard. "I'm Declan O'Hara. I'm the artist featured in this room."

I watched as Alec narrowed his eyes as if sizing up this man, yet he shook his hand anyway.

"I'm Detective Alec Graham with the Locklyn Police Department. This is Ainsley Reynolds."

Declan turned to me and I raised my hand to shake his, but in one swift motion, he'd lifted my hand to his lips. My mouth dropped open and I struggled to stay somewhat cool about this greeting.

Where was this man from? What time period? No boy at school would ever do something so...charming...as kiss a girl's hand at introduction.

"It's nice to meet you, Miss Reynolds."

"It's Ainsley," I said quietly.

"Ainsley," he repeated in his accent. My name vibrated in the air when he repeated it. "Please call me Declan." He glanced between me and Alec as if asking a silent question, but Alec didn't say anything.

"You're the artist of all of these pieces?" I asked, as I slipped a cheese cube into my mouth. I was afraid I might pass out again. Wait until Molly heard about this. Where was she?

Declan surveyed the room. "Yes, I tried to keep the collections together for the exhibit. A few I collaborated on with another artist. This collection here is Celtic-Irish. It was my first collection. My father is from Northern Ireland."

I nodded my head as I nibbled on a cracker. Alec leaned over a framed canvas and studied it further.

Declan continued. "The collection near the fireplace has a Renaissance theme while the ones near the door are Modern Art pieces."

"They are absolutely beautiful, Declan."

He studied my face for a moment. "Thank you. I'm thrilled that you like them."

"Like them? I love them. You're going to make quite a career for yourself," I said.

"That's my plan, but most of these aren't for sale. I take great care when I create them, and I feel they will hang in a museum one day. Not in someone's living room."

"I agree, but it's a shame. I'd love to walk into my living room and see one of these pieces every morning."

Alec gave me a sideways glance and then continued to observe one of the Celtic pieces closest to me. The frame was large, maybe eleven by seventeen inches, from my estimation. It was made from ornately carved wood featuring Celtic crosses at the corners and a set of wings in the middle of the top and bottom of the frame. The wings at the top reminded me of angel's wings with feathers, but the bottom set were more like a bat's wings. The canvas under the glass held a painting of a Celtic cross amid a cemetery. There were gravestones on either side of the cross. It was in a simple black paint or ink, except for the skull with the blooming red rose vine in the bottom right-hand corner.

"You've never sold these frames to anyone? I feel like I've seen something similar recently. Where do you get your ideas?" Alec asked, as he snapped a picture of the piece with his phone.

Declan moved a little closer to the piece. "No, I don't sell them. As for ideas, it depends on my mood. When I went through a dark period in my life, all I could see was images like this in my head. They followed me everywhere, whispering to me, until I finally relented and made art out of them."

I slowly stood up to get a better view of the piece. "Did it work?"

Declan cocked his head.

"Were you able to quiet the voices in your head?"

He studied me for a moment with that look of fascination I'd seen several times today. He turned back to his artwork. "Nothing can do that. It's the curse of the artist. All creatives really. We create to get away from the voices, the whispers, to silence them, and instead immortalize them with our art."

"How do you make these?" Alec asked.

"The artist I worked with used a particular ink and paper for the creations and then mounted them on a treated canvas. I don't make the frames until the piece is mounted and under glass."

"You hand make these frames?" I asked, as I ran my hand over the wooden frame in front of Alec. I clearly was not hiding how impressed I was at this collection.

"Yes, I customize each piece to the art it holds. It might be my favorite part."

I was still admiring Declan's art when Elijah and Molly joined us.

"Declan, I see you've met my guests. Declan and I collaborated on several pieces for the Celtic collection," Elijah said.

"Yes, and it's been a pleasure, but I really must mingle, I suppose. It's expected of us." He nodded toward me. "It was nice to talk with you, Ainsley."

"You too."

Declan and Elijah walked over to an older couple on the other side of the room. My guess was they were donors to the University, or alumni, or both.

"What do you think?" Molly asked quietly.

"About what? The art? It's gorgeous."

Molly rolled her eyes. "Not the art. Declan. I met him in the other room. He reminds me so much of Elijah, so creative. Although he might be a little brooding," she said, as she observed one of his pieces.

"His work is fantastic."

"Yep. And I think he would be perfect for you," Molly said, with that poop-eating grin smeared across her face again.

"Are you feeling any better now that you've eaten?" Alec asked, without looking at me. He was watching Elijah and Declan as they spoke to the guests.

"Yes. I think you were right. Low blood sugar. I need to remember to eat with so much going on."

"What happened?" Molly asked, the smile replaced by a look of concern.

"I'll tell you in the restroom. Do you know where there is one?"

"Sure, I saw some by the elevators."

I touched Alec's arm and he slowly turned his head towards me, but kept his eyes glued to the two men. "We're going to the restroom by the elevators."

Alec nodded, but didn't answer. When I got to the exit door to slip out to the hallway to join Molly, I glanced back at him. He was still staring at the two men and I wondered what was going through his mind.

I gazed past him to Elijah and Declan. Elijah was having an animated conversation with the couple. However, Declan caught my gaze and held it. He grinned as he lifted the cup in his hand as if toasting his achievement.

I left the room when I saw Alec begin to turn his head.

~ ~ ~

I filled Molly in on everything that had happened since she'd left with Elijah. She listened intently as she fixed her updo.

"Glad you're feeling better, but you've got to eat more tonight or you're going to faint again. Maybe we can get Detective Graham to stop at a drive-thru."

"No. I don't want fast food. I can wait until I get home."

Molly watched my reflection in the mirror. "You look beautiful tonight, you know that, right?"

"Thanks, Mol. You do too."

Molly rolled her eyes at me again. "Of course, I do. But what I'm saying is you've been getting a lot of attention from guys lately, and I want to remind you that you don't need to starve yourself."

"I'm not starving myself. I forgot to eat today. There's been a lot going on," I remarked, probably a little too defensively.

Molly put her hands up. "Okay. By the way, Elijah told me that Declan came here from London and managed to catch the eye of every art professor because of his unique talent. Apparently, he can create art in different mediums across the board and everything looks masterful. Declan told Elijah he's been creating art since he was a child. Like a savant."

"Really? Well, I can see that. The pieces in his collection are extraordinary and I didn't get the chance to see his Modern Art pieces up close. Did you notice how Al – Detective Graham – was watching him when we left though? Do you think he doesn't trust him for some reason?"

Molly scrunched up her nose. "I saw him. But then again, he's supposed to watch us and make sure no one snatches us up. From what you said, he left the room and came back to find *you* entertaining a stranger and pawning all over the man's art."

"That is not what I said at all," I laughed.

"I'm surprised he didn't shoot Declan for looking at you like he did," Molly quipped, as she pulled a lip gloss out of her purse to touch up.

"What do you mean?"

"Come on. I know you saw it. I'm your best friend and I saw it from across the room. Declan likes you, but he doesn't have a clue that Detective Graham is a major obstacle."

"How so?" I asked quietly, although I already knew the answer. My crush on him was a major block, so much so, I hadn't noticed Declan's interest.

"Declan was looking at you the way you look at Detective Graham. And here's a little secret I'm going to let you in on as your BFF. Elijah asked me how long the two of you have been going out. I told him you weren't dating each other and that the detective is here on business. He laughed. He can see it in the detective's eyes that he's falling for you. You need to be careful, Ainsley. That's a dangerous game to play with real consequences. He's not just some boy we go to school with every day."

When I didn't answer, she tugged on my scarf. "Anyway, you need to come with me to see Elijah's work."

When we left the restroom, Alec stood near the elevators. He tapped his watch as we approached. "We should think about heading out. It'll take more than an hour to get back."

I nodded my head, but Molly pulled on my arm. "We can, Detective, but let me take Ainsley over to Elijah's art exhibit to show her his work. It was the reason we came, remember?" She pulled me down the hall but waved back at Alec. "You can come, too."

I was keenly aware that Alec was trailing behind us towards Room Number Four. I wondered if Elijah was right about Alec's feelings towards me. Could it be true? Was he here to protect us or was he really here because he *wanted* to be here with me? Did Mom see the same look out of his eyes and that's why she felt the need to remind him that I'm still in high school?

I cleared my head as we entered the room. Although Elijah's work wasn't as masterful as his classmate Declan's in my opinion, the pieces were still amazing. Much better than I could ever do in an Art class.

The majority of his pieces were paintings, although he did have a few sculptures. I'd seen most of these on his website. Paintings of supernatural and mythological creatures from legends. His original painting of "The Demon" was also featured. A shiver ran up my spine. If only people knew the demons were real.

It wasn't until I made my way to the center of the room and the throng of people shifted that I saw the marble statue. It was as horrible and grotesque as the demon in the painting. Its mouth stood open with rows of teeth bared. How could Elijah have managed to cut all of that detail into the stone?

My pulse quickened as the air in the room began to charge again. Why hadn't Elijah told me he'd made a statue of his brother's Muladach? The demon statue had one arm outstretched as if reaching for me. A long index finger, complete with a sharp claw, seemed to point to something unseen in the distance.

I touched the black and white marble stone. Ice cold. I ran my hand over the smoothness of the stone, over the demon's head, around his ears, and down his shoulder to his extended arm. My finger trailed the length of the statue's arm to its fingers. I cupped my hand over its claw as I studied the detail of the creature's face. I knew this statue wasn't alive, but I could feel the electrical charge emanating from it. It was exactly like the creatures I'd seen.

"Ainsley! What are you doing?!" Molly grabbed my hand away from the statue as I realized I'd pressed my palm into the sharp claw. I watched mutely as my blood dripped onto the demon's marble platform. I could barely make out Molly fussing at me and apologizing to the onlookers.

A strong arm grabbed me around the shoulders and began leading me out of the room. It was Alec.

"We're leaving. Now."

~ ~ ~

Alec took me to the SUV and placed me in the front seat as he took his jacket off and tossed it past me to the driver's side door. He walked quickly around to the back and opened the hatch. A few seconds later, he emerged with a First Aid kit and set it down on the floorboard. Once he had a couple of alcohol wipes, tape, and a bandage out, he held his hand out, palm up, for mine.

"Let me see," he demanded.

Reluctantly, I gave him my hand and he wiped the cut on my palm down with the alcohol pads. I refused to cry although it burned something terrible. He leaned against the passenger seat to steady himself as he cleaned the wound. My left knee pressed into his hip near his side arm.

He quietly bandaged my hand and then reached past my knee and slammed the kit closed with his fist. "Good news is the cut isn't deep enough to need stitches. What were you thinking?"

Without warning, I started to cry. My eyes stung as the makeup melted and mixed with the tears. I couldn't answer him because my throat suddenly burned and refused to let any words escape for fear I might sob out loud.

Truth was I didn't know why I had touched the statue. I'd felt the sudden need to be close to it, to touch it. It was almost as if the electrical charge in the air drew me to it.

Finally, I made out the words. "I don't know. I'm sorry."

Alec lowered his head as he exhaled. He was still pressed against my seat with the door open. I knew he had to be tired and I didn't help. If he wasn't sure if I was still a kid, he was certainly convinced now.

He leaned down and cupped my face in his hands as he raised my gaze to meet his. He used his thumbs to wipe at my tears as they fell.

"Don't cry. You can tell me what happened when you calm down." He pushed my hair away from my face as he leaned forward. "I'm not mad," he whispered. His mouth was so close to mine that I wasn't sure if he might kiss me.

With me in the middle of an ugly cry, probably not. But, I instinctively placed my hand on his chest and gripped his shirt, pulling him a little closer. My knee pressed into him.

But, Alec didn't pull away. He searched my eyes as if struggling with something.

"Is she okay?" It was Molly's voice from behind Alec. I immediately let go of his shirt as he let his hands drop. He grabbed the First Aid kit.

"I've got her wound bandaged. It's not deep enough for stitches," he answered her as he walked back to the open hatch to return the kit.

"Where were you?" I asked her, as I turned around in my seat to latch my seatbelt.

"I cleaned up the drops of blood and then told Elijah we had to go."

Alec came over and shut my passenger door and then opened the back door for Molly to get in, but she hesitated.

"Are you okay?" she asked me.

"Yes," I said, as I pulled the mirrored visor down to straighten my makeup. "Let's go home."

~ ~ ~

The three of us didn't speak much on the way home. It was a long drive and I was exhausted. I still didn't have the words to explain to Alec about what drew me to the statue.

He was quiet too and appeared to be in deep thought. Probably about what *could almost* have happened in the parking lot. I snuck a peek at him. He had his elbow resting on the window with his hand on the side of his head and drove with the other hand at the top of the steering wheel. It'd been over two years since I'd kissed a boy, but I knew the look right before they attempted one. Alec had had that look in the SUV as he held my face in his hands. However, I'd also seen a battle raging behind those green eyes.

It was better that we hadn't kissed.

He was trying to do a job and I wasn't making it any easier on him.

We arrived at Molly's house and I told her I'd call her tomorrow. Alec walked her to the door and I watched as they spoke for a moment before Molly waved at me and then went inside.

When Alec pulled back onto the street, I studied his profile lit up from the streetlights as we passed. "I'm sorry about tonight," I started. "It felt like an electrical charge in the air in that last exhibit room. It intensified when I touched the statue. It was like a magnet. I *needed* to touch it. I'm not sure what happened after that."

Alec didn't answer right away.

"Look, Ainsley. You're smart, but you've gotta be more careful. Behaving that way in public will bring too much attention to you and the last thing we want is for the murderer to take notice of you. Especially since you have been at two of the crime scenes."

"You think the killer or killers were there tonight?" I asked, shocked by the idea. "But we were over an hour away from Locklyn."

"I know, but that doesn't mean the murderer lives here or isn't capable of trailing you."

It was my turn not to answer. I hadn't thought about the killer being in Charlotte or at the art show.

Of course, that was why Alec was with me tonight. To protect me and Molly. Elijah had it all wrong.

It was why Alec wasn't home with his girlfriend Kelsey right now. And it was why he'd wrestled with the thought of kissing me.

He pulled up in front of my house, but I opened the SUV door before he could get out of the driver's side. I started up the driveway towards the front door with my house key in my hand.

"Wait."

I heard him but continued up the driveway anyway.

He caught up to me close to the steps and placed his hand on my wrist, encircling it with his thumb and index finger, turning me around to face him. "I said wait, please." He took a deep breath and glanced up at the house. The porch light and a lamp in the living room were the only lights on. I didn't bother mentioning that Mom's room was on the other side of the house and she was probably already in bed.

"You were safe tonight even if things didn't go as planned," he said.

"I know, Alec. I'm just really tired. Tired from a long day and a long evening. Tired of not knowing what's going on in other people's heads."

Alec dropped his hand from my wrist. Maybe he was tired of the same things too.

I bit my lower lip when he didn't answer. "I'll call you tomorrow and try to explain it to you in more detail, okay?"

Alec nodded his head. "Maybe we both need to explain some things tomorrow. Get some rest. Goodnight."

I mumbled goodnight and after I was in the house with the front door locked and alarm reset, I headed for my room. I stripped down in my bathroom and threw on my comfiest pajamas and then washed all the makeup off. It didn't look so bad, but I could tell I'd cried. My eyes were already puffy. Crying meant a mascara disaster, but I'd cleaned most of it off in the truck. I put some moisturizer on my face and climbed into bed with my mind reeling like a projector. What had Alec meant about we *both* needed to explain some things?

More importantly, I needed to figure out why I was drawn to the statue. Was there a creature lurking somewhere in the vicinity? I couldn't help but wonder if one of the event-goers would become the next victim.

I thought about Declan. He was already a tortured artist. I hoped a demon wouldn't make him more so. When I talked with him, it was like talking to a man out of place and time. I could see the intelligence and sorrow behind his dark eyes. Suddenly, I remembered that after I'd fainted, Declan was with me and I'd felt the vibration of energy between us. I hadn't seen any creatures though. Maybe Alec was right, and one had been close.

I decided to tell Alec about the energy charge between Declan and me, although I wasn't sure he would like that news. He'd stared at Declan awfully hard tonight.

But then again, that was his job.

CHAPTER SEVEN

Mom was already in the kitchen by the time I made my way in there the next morning. "You're up earlier than I thought you'd be on a Saturday. What time did you get in?" she asked.

I grabbed a coffee mug from the cabinet and placed it in the Keurig tray. "I think it was around midnight. It's a little over an hour's drive from Charlotte and we dropped Molly off first."

"How'd it go?" she asked, as she handed me the cashew milk from the refrigerator.

"It was nice. Molly's friend Elijah is an exceptional artist. Plus, I met another artist by the name of Declan O'Hara from London. He works with ink and canvas and handcrafts each frame. You've got to see his work sometime. He refuses to sell most of it though. He wants them to hang in museums one day."

"Wow, that's a little presumptuous," Mom commented.

"Maybe. You'd have to see the pieces." I stirred the cashew milk and stevia into my coffee. As soon as I got a job, the first thing I was going to buy was real creamer. I joined Mom at the dining table. "Where's Ben? Still in bed?"

"Yes. I let him play Fortnite until after ten last night. What happened to your hand?" she asked, suddenly alarmed.

I'd forgotten all about it although the bandage was neatly wrapped across the back of my hand. "Oh, I accidently cut it on a statue last night. Detective Graham had a First Aid kit. He didn't think it required stitches or anything." I shrugged and hoped the gesture conveyed she had nothing to worry about.

"How did Detective Graham like the art show?"

"I guess he did. He kind of stayed on guard all evening. He trailed behind us most of the time."

Mom seemed satisfied with that answer. "Ben is going to spend the day at Gavin's, so I'll be in my office. What are your plans for the day?"

I immediately thought of Alec. "I'll head over to Molly's. We might hit up some of the stores again about applications. No one has called me for an interview yet."

"I would have thought someone would have by now. Call the gym and ask for the owner. Maybe he hasn't had time to call. I'm headed to work until Ben gets up. Don't forget to eat breakfast."

After thinking about what I would say to Alec about Declan, I decided to skip breakfast to get the day started early.

~ ~ ~

I showered quickly and pulled on a pair of black leggings and black ankle boots. I found my black and purple Victoria Secret's Bombshell pushup bra in the closet to wear under my plaid purple and black long button-up flannel shirt. I loved this one because it was by far one of my favorites since the shirt came with a belt that highlighted my waist. I turned in front of the floor-length mirror. It was true that I wished my hips were smaller, but with the belt creating a defined waist it gave my curves an hour-glass figure. I decided to go with full-face makeup and blown-out hair, since I really did plan to revisit some of the stores and talk to the managers. I threw on a puffy black sleeveless vest and glanced at myself one more time in the mirror as I popped a piece of gum into my mouth and removed the bandage from my palm.

I'd decided to tell Alec about Declan face-to-face.

I wasn't sure if he'd be home on a Saturday morning or already at the station, but I decided it didn't matter. It was a warmer October morning and I wanted to walk. The forecast on my phone showed the temperature high today could reach 69 degrees.

One great thing about living in Locklyn was the sidewalks. You could walk about anywhere in town with the family-friendly sidewalks and neighborhoods. As I breathed the fresh Fall air in deeply, I suddenly had the feeling someone was watching me. I slowed my pace, but didn't see anyone. An occasional car would drive by at the speed limit of 25 miles per hour, but no one slowed down. I finally decided it was probably a nosy old lady peering out from behind her curtains.

It didn't take me too long to reach Alec's street and as I approached, I noticed the SUV parked out front.

Good, he's home.

As I drew closer, my mind began to race. What if Kelsey was there? Alec hadn't been too happy to see me at his house last time. Would he be angry? Would he send me away without hearing me out? Was Rowan Wesley lurking down the street?

I glanced around, and although I noticed a silver diesel truck that looked vaguely familiar and a neighbor who had just parked in front of the house across the street, I was confident that Rowan was nowhere in sight and if Kelsey answered the door, I would wing it.

With my thoughts reeling, I stepped up to his porch, opened the glass door, and knocked on Detective Graham's front door, totally prepared to see Kelsey's face and Ugg boots.

Alec opened the door but didn't appear surprised to see me. I, on the other hand, almost dropped my gum out of my mouth. And it wasn't from the smell of bacon cooking as it wafted through his house either.

He had on a pair of jeans. That was it. No shirt, no socks. He leaned on the doorway with his tattooed forearm while he held a coffee mug in his other hand. When I'd seen him yesterday, morning fresh from his shower, I'd only thought his body was cut. Today it was as if he had an early morning audition for a *300* sequel.

"Why am I not surprised to see you this morning?" He didn't wait for my answer as he stepped out onto the front porch. He leaned against the brick and concrete bannister that faced the street and took a drink from his mug before he turned to look at me. "Gorgeous," he breathed, as he set the mug down on the bannister. "It's a gorgeous morning." Alec leaned against the brick.

My stomach audibly growled. Freaking bacon.

"What are you doing here?" he asked, but he didn't look mad that I stood on his porch. Or, disappointed.

"I was on my way to Molly's house...and smelled bacon," I said and smiled.

He smiled before he took another sip from his mug, but I noticed he very subtly observed my outfit from head to toe and back again. When he set the mug down again, he stretched. Was he doing this on purpose? Every muscle under his skin rippled and I felt the heat rush into my cheeks.

Suddenly, he grabbed his mug and started for the door and I wondered if Kelsey was inside.

"Well, come on, before you make me burn something. Sounds like you're hungry."

He held the glass door open for me as I slid past his bare chest. I followed him into the living room and I shut the door behind me as he continued to the back of the house. I dropped my crossbody bag on his couch and slowly followed the scent from the cooked bacon. The next room was a dining room with only a table and four chairs in the middle. I slid off my vest and hung it on the back of one of the oak chairs. A bathroom was directly across from the table near a large doorway that led to the kitchen. As I maneuvered around the table to my right was a room which had to be the master bedroom. I could see a king size bed facing the door with a chest of drawers to its right. The blankets were still ruffled as if Alec had got up not too long ago. Or, maybe he never made his bed.

For a man who lived alone, the kitchen was huge. It had a step down into the kitchen portion with the appliances and counters and another step down that led to the other half of the room which contained a small table with two chairs near a window, a washer and dryer against the short free-standing wall that separated the kitchen from the eating area, and a backdoor.

"How do you like your eggs?" he asked.

"Oh, you don't have to. I was joking. I came to talk to you about last night."

"I could hear your stomach growling from across the porch. If you don't tell me, then scrambled it is."

"Scrambled is fine. Thanks," I leaned against the counter top directly behind Alec as he made the eggs. The plate of cooked bacon was on the stove. From this viewpoint, I could see the detail in his tattoo which took up most of his back. It was a demon of some type although different from the creatures I'd seen this week. Its horns started at the base of Alec's neck while its wings stretched out across his shoulder blades. Its body was encircled by a robe that seemed to bellow in the wind. Its clawed feet and the end of a tail reached to his lower back and it seemed to move as he moved. It was an impressive piece of art. The tattoo along with his bulging muscles was what made Alec underneath his shirts.

My stomach growled again.

Alec turned with the spatula in his hand. A little smirk played on his lips.

Busted.

"What?" he asked.

"Hmmm?"

"Molly lives in the opposite direction from here. You didn't drive unless you picked up a silver truck since yesterday, so you must have walked. And you didn't call or text to talk about last night. So, what is it?"

He turned to stir the eggs, so I took a few steps and stood beside him. I watched him add in a small bowl of diced green bell peppers and tomatoes.

"I like your tattoo," I said quietly.

He paused in his stirring. "You're standing really close," he whispered.

"Oh, I'm sorry." I took a couple of steps away from him. He resumed his stirring of the egg mixture. Did I make him feel uncomfortable? "I was thinking about Declan last night," I started.

His jaw clenched as he motioned for me to hand him the shredded cheese. "Why?"

"I don't know how to explain it. It's why I didn't text you. It's too much to convey in a text. That day at the junior high when Molly and I found the woman's body, I felt an electrical charge. I told you I felt it again last night in front of the statue. What I didn't tell you was I felt something similar when I met Declan. The air between us charged. I'm wondering if he's going to be the next victim."

Alec frowned. He took a step backwards away from me and grabbed the plate of bacon. "Hmm," was all he said.

I followed him to the kitchen table. "Hmm? That's it?"

I watched as he went back up to the stove and removed two plates from one of the cabinets. "I don't know what to say, Ainsley. This whole situation is beyond normal police work. Sometimes we use mediums on cases, but this is outside of that too."

He split the scrambled eggs onto the plates and carried them to the table. "Even with the dark mist on that surveillance, it doesn't prove you are seeing demons or that something supernatural is involved with these murders, although I do think you see *something*." He went back for forks and glasses. "Can you grab the orange juice from the refrigerator, or do you want coffee?"

"Orange juice is fine."

Alec left the kitchen as I poured the juice into our glasses and added a slice of bacon to my plate. The food smelled wonderful and I was starved. Come to think of it, I hadn't eaten since the art exhibit last night. And that was only crackers and cheese cubes.

Alec came back wearing a gray tee-shirt.

Great. Not only do I make him feel uncomfortable, but now he's self-conscious with me here.

"Do you want some toast?" he asked.

"No, this is great. Thanks."

He took a bite of eggs and watched me for a moment, "When was the last time you ate?"

"Last night when you brought me those cheese and crackers."

"That's what I thought. You know, last night you told me what your father taught you about finding a guy who will value you, not just want you. Well, I'd like to add that it's important you value yourself too."

"Meaning?" I asked quietly.

"That you take care of yourself first. Remember to eat. Not walk about town alone with a killer on the loose. Not falling for guys like Declan O'Hara," he concluded, as he took a bite of his bacon.

I sat back in the chair, stunned.

"Oh-kay," I said slowly. "I understand your first two points, but what's wrong with Declan?"

He leaned forward with a little smile on his lips. "You told me you felt a charge when you met him. Are you sure it wasn't tension? Attraction?" He raised an eyebrow.

"Really?" I asked, as I cocked my head. "Just because I haven't dated in two years doesn't mean I don't know the difference between attraction and a shift in the atmosphere. I'm not going to lie. There was definitely a little bit of tension and attraction last night. And not just between Declan and me."

My last remark wiped the smile off his face.

He broke eye contact first. "I overstepped. Last night and this morning. I shouldn't have said anything about Declan." He stood up and grabbed his plate. "I'm heading into the station for a while to see where we are in the case. Let me give you a lift to Molly's house."

I cleared my dishes and followed him to the dishwasher. "That's okay. I can walk."

"I'd prefer you didn't for the many reasons I cited." He took my plate and stuck it in the machine and closed the door.

For a moment, he stood there as if he wanted to say something but didn't. With the dishwasher shut, he stood closer than he'd allowed earlier at the stove. Would he remark that I was standing too close again?

"Why did you say you overstepped last night?" I asked quietly.

"Ainsley," his voice came out husky, as he glanced down at my shirt and then back up to my eyes. He shook his head. "You're driving me crazy. If you only knew." He backed away from me and turned towards the dining room. "I'm getting my shoes and then we're leaving."

Alec went into his bedroom and shut the door, so I walked slowly back to the living room to get my purse and wait for him by the door.

"I'm driving him crazy," I whispered to myself. What did that mean? Was I annoying him? I decided to never invite myself over to Alec's house again. I smiled at my reflection in the mirror beside the front door to check for any hidden eggs and bacon until I realized my shirt was unbuttoned at the top. I could see my cleavage.

Crap. No wonder Alec had practically panted over my chest in that husky voice. He probably thought I'd done it on purpose. Kudos to the push-up bra manufacturers. It'd done its job well.

I started to button it, but decided the heck with it. If he thought I was like that, then he wouldn't believe me if I told him any differently.

Then again, why was I making things difficult for him?

Alec walked into the living room and while he holstered his gun, I quietly buttoned that darn button. He grabbed his ball cap, wallet, and keys from the coffee table and looped his badge around his neck on a lanyard. Apparently, he didn't have to wear a suit today.

"You ready?" he asked, but I noticed he looked directly at my shirt.

Great. Now he does think I had it unbuttoned on purpose.

I fought the urge to sigh. "Yes, absolutely."

We stepped out onto the front porch and I waited as Alec locked the door. It was already warmer than it had been just an hour ago. He turned and held his arm out for me to go down the steps first. As we walked to the SUV, I noticed a couple standing on the sidewalk a few houses away. The guy had turned quickly towards the girl and was holding her, but I'd recognized her.

Rowan Wesley.

The guy planted a kiss on Rowan's lips. At least if she was kissing this dude, then she wouldn't see me leave Alec's house…again.

Alec opened the passenger door for me, but I paused as I caught a glimpse of the couple in the side mirror. The boy had moved away from Rowan who was now holding her phone up with a smirk on her face. I peered a little closer in the mirror before turning to face him.

It was Derek. Bronwyn's boyfriend.

~ ~ ~

I stood still, completely stunned that Derek was the guy I'd seen kissing Rowan. Derek was already on the move and climbed into the silver diesel truck. I knew it was familiar. I'd only seen Derek in his dad's truck twice.

I turned around to Alec as he placed his hand on my lower back to help me into the SUV. He cocked his head as if confused by my hesitation.

I felt the pressure from his hand as it moved to my hip. I couldn't tell him about what Rowan had said at school. And not only had she'd seen me again, Derek had confirmed Rowan's sighting.

I heard Derek start the engine of his truck as I climbed into the passenger side. Derek and I made eye contact as he passed the SUV. I was speechless as I glanced into the side mirror and watched as Rowan sashayed back to her bat cave.

Why would Derek cheat on Bronwyn with Rowan, of all people? As far as I knew all of my friends despised her and steered clear of her and her Rowanites.

Apparently not Derek.

How could I tell Bronwyn without confirming the rumors around school?

"Are you okay? You're white as a sheet," Alec said, after he climbed in and started the truck.

I swallowed hard. "Yeah. It's just that guy who passed in the truck. He's dating my friend Bronwyn."

Alec adjusted the rearview mirror. "And I take it that girl isn't Bronwyn?"

"No, she's not. She's a spiteful, vindictive chick named Rowan Wesley. She's a troublemaker. And she really doesn't like me."

I was quiet on the drive to Molly's house. I couldn't tell Alec about the confrontation with Rowan about him. He'd never have anything to do with me again.

Alec let me out of the SUV and I mumbled a thanks for the breakfast and the ride.

Apparently, Molly had seen me pull up because she had the door open before I reached the porch. She waved at Alec as he pulled off before lowering her voice to address me. "What is this? Are you two an actual couple now?"

"No. I went to his house this morning to talk to him about the case and he offered to drop me off on his way to the station."

I slipped my shoes off in Molly's foyer and left them in the shoe tray.

"Mol, I saw something today and I'm not sure what I should do about it."

Molly motioned for me to follow her into the kitchen, "What did you see? Was it another one of those creatures?"

"No, not that one, but a creature nonetheless. I came out of Alec's house and saw Rowan Wesley kissing a guy on the sidewalk a couple of houses away."

Molly laughed as she handed me a Dr. Pepper. "So? Everyone's kissed Rowan. She sleeps around."

I placed the can of soda back in the refrigerator and grabbed a bottle of water instead.

"So, the guy was Derek."

Molly stopped laughing and stared dumbfounded at me. "Are you sure? Why would he cheat on Bronwyn?"

"It was definitely him. He was driving his dad's silver truck." I took a drink of water. "I don't know why he'd cheat on her, but he was staring at me pretty hard yesterday. I'd chalked it up to Rowan's rumor. Should we tell Bronwyn?"

"Uh, yeah. I'd want to know if my boyfriend was cheating on me. Wouldn't you?"

I thought about Alec, although he wasn't my boyfriend. He hadn't mentioned Kelsey at all this morning.

"Molly, she saw me coming out of Alec's house and she had her phone. You know what she accused me of Friday. What if she makes this a big deal?"

"Let her try. You're not sleeping with that detective. Say you stopped by to tell him something about the case and that was it. He was on his way out the door anyway."

When I didn't answer right away, Molly leaned over the kitchen counter until she was inches from my face. "You're not sleeping with that detective, right?"

I met her stare. "No," I said, as I thought about our almost kiss last night and about how he'd whispered that I was driving him crazy in that husky voice this morning. I thought about his badge and his career.

"Absolutely not," I answered, as I took another drink of water.

I decided it was best to limit my time with Alec until all of this got sorted out with Bronwyn and Derek.

~ ~ ~

Molly called Bronwyn and asked if we could come over this morning. At first, Bronwyn bucked and complained that she had too much to do. She'd promised her mother she'd help clean the house. Bronwyn's mother was older and nine months pregnant with her fifth baby due any day now. Bronwyn said her mother got out of breath easily and had to rest more this time around.

"I know," Molly agreed, after Bronwyn filled her in with everything she had to get done. "Maybe we could come over and help you? There's something Ainsley and I need to tell you. It's important," she paused and met my eyes before she continued. "It's about Derek."

"Derek?" Bronwyn asked loud enough, that I could hear it over Molly's iPhone without the speaker on.

"Yes."

Bronwyn told Molly to come on over, but to come to the back door because she was sweeping and mopping the floors and she could talk to us on the porch.

"Bronwyn also said not to get your feelings hurt if her mother says anything to you. She's nesting and in a mood."

I nodded my head as I knew what Bronwyn meant. She was the oldest and we'd all been friends for a long time. I'd witnessed her mother's other pregnancies as the youngest was only two. Bronwyn shouldered a great deal of responsibility as her father was the only wage earner and her mother chased after three other children.

Molly drove us to Bronwyn's house right past the city limits. The two-story farmhouse was set apart from other houses on the road and her parents owned close to two hundred acres, mostly wooded, behind the house. The land that was clear gave the children a safe place to play.

Molly parked in front of the house and we walked around back. The screened-in porch was wide and L-shaped, and it covered the entire back side of the house and part of the side. The screen door was unlocked, so we let ourselves onto the porch. The wooden planks creaked, and Bronwyn stuck her head around the open back door.

"Hey, I'm coming. I'm almost done with the kitchen floor," she yelled, as her head disappeared.

"No problem," Molly answered her, as we sat down in the rocking chairs. Bronwyn's mother had turned the back side of the house into a quiet sanctuary with four rockers lined up and little white tables separating each one. The children kept their toys in totes around the corner.

Neither one of us spoke as we waited for our friend. I thought Molly must feel the same anxiety I did. Bronwyn was extremely territorial anyway and I'd caught Derek red-handed. But should I tell her about how he'd eye-balled me yesterday?

Bronwyn came out to the porch. "Hey, sorry about that. Mom can't do heavy cleaning right now and keep up with the kids." She sat down in one of the rockers and scooted it to face us. "Now what was it you were saying about Derek?"

I felt Molly's eyes on me, so I leaned forward slightly in the chair and answered. "I was at a friend's house on Lanier Lane this morning and saw Derek."

"Okay," Bronwyn said slowly.

"He wasn't alone. He was with Rowan Wesley."

"Rowan? What do you mean, he was with Rowan?"

"Bronwyn, Ainsley saw Derek kiss Rowan on the sidewalk before he got into his dad's truck and drove away. He looked right at her."

Bronwyn blinked several times. I'd always thought Bronwyn was the prettiest girl in school with her exotic hair and skin. Right now, that tanned complexion was red.

Bronwyn turned her dark eyes on me. "You're lying. Why would Derek cheat on me? And with Rowan?"

"I'm not. Why would I lie to you?"

Bronwyn raised herself slowly from the rocker, her hands balled into tight fists, her face full of contempt aimed in my direction. I leaned back in the chair. Was she going to hit me?

"You're jealous because you don't have a boyfriend like Derek. All you've had is your sad little life with your mom and brother. No wonder that rumor about the cop is going around. You're suddenly so thirsty for any man's attention."

I stood up, but Molly squeezed between me and the outraged Bronwyn.

"That's enough, Bronwyn," Molly said. "It's the truth and Ainsley's not the only one that saw them together. Detective Graham was there too."

Bronwyn walked around to the back of her rocker, her eyes darted all over the place before they landed on me again.

"So, you and your cop boyfriend saw Derek with Rowan?" she asked.

"He's not my boyfriend," I said, probably a little too quickly. "I was there to tell him something about the case when I saw them."

"I think you two should go home now. I have a lot to think about." She moved the rocker back to its original position and slowly started for the kitchen door.

"Are you sure, Bronwyn? We came here not just to tell you, but to support you with whatever you want to do," Molly called after her.

Bronwyn stopped at the kitchen door with her hand on the knob. "I'm fine. Go home," she said, and shut the door behind her.

"I feel ridiculously bad. We did do the right thing, right?" I asked Molly, before she started the car.

"Yes, we did the right thing," Molly answered, frowning as she turned the key. "Bronwyn is hurt and probably feels betrayed by Derek, angry at Rowan, and embarrassed because we are the ones who told her. We need to give her some time to calm down. She knows we'll support her no matter what."

"Do we wait to check on her? Or, call her tonight?"

Molly frowned again as she glanced at the farmhouse in the rearview mirror. "If I don't hear from her by tomorrow evening, I'll call her," Molly turned to look at me before starting the car out of Bronwyn's long driveway. "You know, she didn't mean those things about you. She's angry and needed to take it out on someone and you were the messenger."

"I know. I'm not worried about it." But I was worried. I was worried about the consequences of telling Bronwyn and outing Rowan and Derek. If I'd only seen them anywhere else in town instead of on Alec's street.

~ ~ ~

I convinced Molly to drop me off at the gym, so I could find the owner, Henry. I hoped Mom was right and Henry was just busy and hadn't had time to call me yet. The gym wasn't far from home and I told her I'd walk when I was finished. Alec would probably kill me if he knew.

I checked my top button on my shirt as I'd noticed it kept coming undone. That's all I needed was for Henry to think I was hitting on him. Apparently, I loved feeding the rumor mill.

A tall man stood behind the counter dressed in a tee shirt and jeans. He didn't look like any of the other gym goers currently working out with the heavy weights. I noticed he was leaner than Alec, although the man's arms were defined. Maybe the gym had already hired this man as the receptionist.

"May I help you?" he asked. As he smiled down at me, one of his black curls toppled down onto his forehead.

"Hi, I dropped off an application the other day for the receptionist position and I wondered if it had been filled. Or, if I could speak to the owner, possibly?" I asked, as I gave him my biggest smile. After my morning contending with Alec, Rowan, Derek, and Bronwyn, it was the only feature I had left that wouldn't betray the anxiety I felt.

He leaned on the counter and crossed his arms. "Ah. You must be Ainsley," he said with a twinkle in his eye.

"I take it my mother already talked to you about my application," I sighed, biting my lower lip. Leave it to Mom to smother me from across town.

"No, actually, my friend Alec handed me your application the other day. He texted me last night and asked if I'd called you yet." He chuckled as he shook his head. I wasn't sure what to make of his reaction. Or, the fact that Alec had asked him.

"Come on. I'll interview you right now." He glanced around at the current members in the gym and then led me to a door past the large gym mirror. The door opened to a narrow hallway with only three rooms. Two doors were open across from each other, but the door at the end of the hallway was closed. I peeked into the room on the right, apparently a small break room. The man turned into the room on the left.

He walked behind a desk and motioned for me to sit in one of the chairs across from him. "I'm Henry Locke, by the way. I own this gym." He reached across the desk and shook my hand. He was much younger than I'd anticipated for the owner, probably in his thirties.

"Ainsley Reynolds," I answered, and then felt immensely stupid. He already knew who I was.

Henry smiled as he sorted through a file of applications until he pulled mine out. "Here we go," he said as he scanned over it.

My eyes darted around the office as I waited. The wall behind him was full of family and vacation pictures. The shelf to the right held a collection of trophies and medals, but I couldn't read how they were earned.

"Highest education? It says Locklyn High. I assume you're still in school?"

"I graduate in the spring. Then I plan to go to college, probably for the Fall term if everything works out with the financial aspect," I answered. "I'm eligible for a few grants from the military because my father served."

"What do you want to major in?" he asked.

"Elementary education. I'm great with children."

"Well, that's good to know. I may need to hire you as a babysitter in the future," he said and laughed. "My wife and I had a baby two months ago." He pointed to a group of photos on the wall of an infant.

"Oh, congratulations!" I decided right then that I liked Henry.

"I don't want this job to interfere with your school assignments at all. I would need you to work a few evenings a week and probably most Saturdays and every other Sunday. We close at ten o'clock and reopen at six, except for Sundays. Do you think you could balance that with school? It doesn't give you a lot of free time."

"I don't see it as being a problem. My mother would probably appreciate knowing I'm either here or at school."

"Great," he said, and laughed again. "Normally, I pay ten dollars an hour for the receptionist position and you can work out for free when you're not scheduled. There's a 90-day review period and if everything works out, then you'll receive a dollar raise."

"Sounds good."

"Good," he said. "Can you come Tuesday after school for an orientation? It will only take about an hour to watch a video and complete the paperwork. Then you could start Friday."

"Absolutely."

Henry walked me out front as he resumed his spot behind the counter. "Oh, before I forget. Do you want me to schedule you for Saturday evenings? I figured you'd want to workout with Alec and he's usually here in the early afternoons on Saturdays unless he's at work."

"Oh no, no, that's okay," I stammered. "You can schedule me anytime on the weekends. I'll workout around that schedule."

"Oh, okay. I meant I don't have a problem scheduling you around working out with your friends or our classes. My wife teaches Pilates and kickboxing classes if you want to do those. Here's the flyers about what we offer. See you Tuesday!" He turned to help a man who'd walked in.

I read the flyers as I walked quickly home to tell Mom about my new job. Part of me wanted to text Alec and thank him for bringing my name up to Henry last night, but I refused. He was working this case and needed to focus.

The closer I got to my street, I began to feel as if I were being watched again. There was no one on the sidewalks or in their yards. I scanned each house as I continued towards mine - the feeling intensified, a suffocating presence. It felt like someone was charging towards me. I whirled around in front of the mailbox to face it.

There was nothing there. And yet, there was something there. In front of me, beside me.

Behind me. More than one.

I couldn't see them, but I could feel their overwhelming evil. I could hear their breathing.

"Muladach," I whispered, as tears sprang to my eyes.

Suddenly, the air around me filled with snarls from the unseen creatures. Why couldn't I see them this time? I ran at a sprint to the front door and banged on it. I didn't have time to fish out my key.

By the time Mom opened the door, I was a crumpled mess of tears and makeup on the porch. The Muladach were gone.

The neighborhood was quiet again.

~ ~ ~

The next morning, I woke up with a crick in my neck. Probably from trying to get away from the Muladach. Mom had helped me up from the porch, but I'd been unable to tell her what had happened until I was seated in the living room. And then, I couldn't tell her the truth.

In the end, I told her I'd had an anxiety attack thinking about Dad while walking home from the gym. Of course, she was concerned, but I was able to convince her I would be fine with some rest. I'd retreated to my room for the remainder of the day. I'd wrestled with the thought of calling Alec about the Muladach, but I hadn't actually seen them this time and I was drained from yesterday morning's confrontations. Maybe I would call him this afternoon. A phone call wouldn't hurt anything, and Rowan would never know.

Now I was starved. My stomach rumbled out loud, so I made my way into the kitchen. I opened the refrigerator, but nothing looked appealing, so I tried the pantry cabinet. Mom came into the kitchen with her hair up in her rather large pineapple bun again.

"Hey, how are you feeling this morning?" she asked, as she bounced around making herself coffee.

"Better. I'm hungry, but nothing sounds good," I answered, still peering into the cabinet. I finally shut the door, feeling defeated.

"Ben asked for pancakes. Why don't you try to eat some of those? We're having pizza for dinner tonight from your favorite place," she said, as she got out the ingredients to make batter. Neither pancakes or pizza sounded good, but regardless I needed to eat.

"That sounds great, Mom. Thanks."

I made myself a cup of coffee as Mom mixed the batter and I'd taken my first sip when the doorbell rang.

"Who could that be on a Sunday morning?" Mom asked.

"I'll get it," I said, as I headed to the door.

Please be Alec. No, don't be Alec. That could be bad right now because of Rowan and Derek. Never mind. Please be Alec.

I shook my head to clear my thoughts before I opened the door. A FedEx delivery driver stood on the other side of the screen door with a package in his hand. Was Mom expecting a package today? On Sunday?

I opened the screen door.

"Hi. Is this the Reynolds' residence?"

"Yes, it is," I said as I nodded slowly.

The FedEx man handed me the thin box, which was surprisingly heavier than it looked, with his electronic device on top. "I need you to sign for it please."

I used the stylus pen to write my name illegibly as I made a comment about the impossibility of writing anything with these machines. The delivery driver smiled and thanked me. Apparently, he heard that complaint all day long.

I carried the box to the dining table. It wasn't a package for Mom. It was my name printed on the label. I checked the return address. It was blank, but the postage sticker showed it shipped from Charlotte.

Elijah or Declan, maybe? I didn't think Elijah would send me anything.

I hadn't spoken to Declan since the art exhibit Friday night and didn't expect to anytime soon. He was a classmate of Elijah's, not a close friend. In order for him to ship anything to me for delivery on a Sunday from FedEx must have cost him a fortune. If it was from him.

"What's that?" Mom asked from the kitchen.

"I don't know. Would you hand me a knife?"

Mom handed me the paring knife from the butcher's block and watched as I slid it across the tape. The thin box was filled with packing peanuts and bubble wrap. I reached in and touched something hard. I slid it out onto the table.

Without removing the carefully wrapped bubble wrap, I could tell it was a piece of artwork.

I glanced at Mom before I unwrapped it and held it up by its dark cherry wood frame. The frame was ornately carved with vines in painstaking detail. No doubt a handcrafted work by Declan. The picture under the glass was one of the most beautiful I'd ever seen. It was probably from his Celtic collection although I didn't remember seeing this work. It featured a woman with her back to the artist as she sat in front of a pond. Her long blonde hair was coarsely held in a braid that reached to the rock where she sat. In the middle of the pond, emerged a Celtic cross, surrounded by drooping trees. It gave the piece a sorrowful feel even though Declan had used brighter colors of greens, blues, oranges, and browns.

"Oh my," Mom breathed. I'd forgotten she was standing there.

"Remember that artist I told you about at the exhibit? The one with the canvases and hand-carved frames? I think this is from him."

"It's gorgeous," Mom said. "No wonder he wants his work displayed in museums. What does the plaque say?"

"Hmm?'

"The plaque on the back."

I carefully turned the heavy frame over to see a silver plaque screwed into the back.

It read: *Ainsley.*

"He named the piece after me?"

Mom took the frame from my hands as she read the back. "You just met him Friday night? Well, you must have made quite the impression on the young man. Not to mention, the expense of having this special delivered today. Where do you want to hang it?" she asked, as she looked around the dining area.

"I don't know. Declan told me he didn't want his work hanging in people's living rooms, but I'd told him I personally would love to wake up and see his art in my house."

"Well, he took you seriously. Find a place in your room then and I'll help you hang it. Come on, breakfast is ready." She set the frame down on one end of the table.

As I cleared the table of the box and packing material, my mind went in all directions. How could I thank Declan for such an amazing gift?

After breakfast, Mom helped me hang the artwork in my room next to my dresser, so I could see it every morning when I woke up. I snapped a picture of it to show Molly tomorrow.

In the afternoon, I found myself constantly thinking about calling Alec about the Muladach. I hadn't seen them per se, but I'd felt them, and I wondered if another victim would be found soon. If there was a way to stop them before they used someone to kill again, then didn't I have a responsibility to report the presence of the creatures?

Finally, I gave in and pressed the call button on my phone next to his name. The phone rang three times before he picked up.

"Now's not a good time, Ainsley," he answered in a low voice.

"Oh." I should've known he was probably at work or on a crime scene.

"Is that her? Hmm?" I heard what sounded like Kelsey's voice come over the phone. "Well, tell your little girlfriend she left her jacket!"

I automatically reached up to my pajama shirt as I remembered my puffy sleeveless black vest. I'd taken it off at Alec's house yesterday and hung it on the back of a dining room chair. It'd been so warm when we left, I'd totally forgotten about it.

"Oh, I'm sorry. I forgot all about it." I started to say more, but wasn't sure what to say. Apparently, Kelsey had found my vest and she was flipping out. I could hear a string of expletives from her in the background. Several of them were highly descriptive adjectives with me as the proper noun.

"I need to go," Alec said, before he hung up.

I sat on the bed with my hand over my mouth. What had I done? I'd caused a rift between Alec and Kelsey. How could I have been so stupid as to leave my vest there? He must not have told her I'd been back to the house until she found it. A fact that would've made him look guilty in her eyes. This was bad, and I couldn't think of a way to fix it. Kelsey didn't sound like she was in the mood to listen to my explanation either.

If I had any more information about the case, then I'd better tell Detective Tudor.

My phone vibrated in my hand and for a second, I hoped it was Alec. It was an unknown number. After a moment's hesitation, I answered.

"Is this Ainsley?" The voice came over in a very British accent.

"Declan?" I asked, a bit startled.

"Hi, I hope I'm not bothering you. I got your number from Elijah Moore."

"Declan, yes. I received your artwork today. Thank you. It's absolutely beautiful and exquisite. I hung it in my room across from the windows, so I can see it when I wake up. The canvas and frame are extraordinary," I said, as I crossed the room to stand in front of the piece. "It was such a surprise. I don't know how to thank you."

"I'm not sure what artwork you're talking about. I didn't send you anything, but it does sound like a piece from our collection. Maybe Elijah sent it to you. But you can thank me instead of him. Go out with me."

"Go out? Like on a date?" I asked, as I stared at my open-mouthed reflection in the dresser mirror.

"Yes, like a proper date. Let me take you out on Wednesday evening. Dinner, movie, strolling through a park. You name it."

"Declan," I didn't know what to say. I thought about the horrible situation I'd caused for Alec and Kelsey. Maybe going out with someone else was the answer. And it wasn't like Declan was hard on the eyes.

"Unless, of course, you're involved with someone else?"

"Declan, I would love to go out with you on Wednesday," I said, ignoring his last question. We set a time of when he would pick me up from home Wednesday evening. At least, if I had a relationship with Declan, maybe the rumors would die down about Alec and me.

~ ~ ~

Monday morning came too soon after the eventful weekend. I called Molly Sunday night, but she still hadn't spoken to Bronwyn and when she'd called her house, her mother told her she was napping.

I filled Molly in on Declan's gift and our upcoming date. I intentionally left out the part about Alec and Kelsey. I didn't need an I-told-you-so retort from Molly.

"I wonder where he got your address? Elijah didn't ask me for it," Molly frowned.

"I don't know." I hadn't considered how he knew where I lived. I decided I would ask him Wednesday.

As we entered the hallway that led to the cafeteria, we heard a commotion. Bronwyn's shrill voice carried over the oohing and aahing of the crowd gathered in front of the doors.

"Liar! You are such a liar, Derek Killian! Ainsley saw you and Rowan. And so did other people!"

Molly pushed through the crowd with me on her heels. We finally reached the front in time to see a red-face Bronwyn holding back tears as she confronted Derek. Derek stood a few feet away with his hands up.

His voice was barely a whisper. "B, let me explain…"

"Let you explain? Explain what, Derek? Did you fall into Rowan's face?" The crowd erupted into laughter except for Bronwyn, Derek, Molly, and me.

As if on cue, Rowan and her friends pushed to the front of the crowd. Bronwyn spotted her right away.

"And you! Are you not happy sleeping with every other boy in our graduating class, so you have to go after Derek?" Bronwyn was so angry, she was shaking.

Rowan made a face at her accuser and stepped forward. "Derek helped me Saturday and I proved something to him. That's all."

"Helped you? Helped you?!" Bronwyn's voice was as high-pitched as any opera singer as she screamed at Rowan.

Derek ran his hands through his hair, clearly perplexed. The crowd quieted down as Bronwyn moved dangerously close to Rowan's face.

"Yes. He was helping me stake out the detective's house. If anyone is sleeping around, it's your friend Ainsley Reynolds," Rowan spewed out the words as she waved her hand in my direction.

I stopped breathing.

Derek glanced at me before he took another step toward Bronwyn. "B, I swear. That's the only reason I was there. Rowan said the rumor was true, but I didn't believe it until I saw them come out of his house a half hour later."

Rowan smirked as she turned in my direction. "You two must be pretty good together. He couldn't keep his hands off you," she hissed.

The crowd murmured, and some made noises. Before I realized what I was doing, I stepped forward and punched Rowan square in the face with every bit of strength I had.

The blow knocked Rowan backwards and she landed on her knees in front of Derek, who threw his arms up as if to shield her from my wrath. I glared at the two of them.

"You both are liars and deserve every bit of the Hell you are going to get," I seethed.

Molly grabbed my arm and jerked me away from the crowd so hard I almost tripped over my Converse.

Bronwyn grabbed my other arm. "We need to go now."

I tried to shake them off. I'd never felt such rage towards people in my whole life.

However, we didn't get far before Vice-Principal Clendenin stepped in front of us. "My office. Now," he growled, before he barked orders to a student to get the nurse for Rowan.

~ ~ ~

Within a half hour, Molly, Bronwyn, Derek, Rowan, and me sat in Mr. Clendenin's office. Everyone's parents had been called and Rowan held an ice pack up to her nose. Mr. Clendenin suggested that her parents take her to the hospital for an x-ray to make sure it wasn't broken.

In my opinion, her nose was broken. And it served her right, although Mom was going to be furious because we would probably have to pay for Rowan's medical bills. *I* would have to pay them.

Mr. Clendenin took his time as he asked each one of us what occurred this morning and dared any of us to interrupt. He started with Derek who told him that he and Bronwyn were in an argument when things escalated.

Mr. Clendenin asked Bronwyn what the argument was over. "Derek was seen kissing Rowan on Saturday. He and I have been dating for a couple of years."

The Vice-Principal raised an eyebrow as he glanced between Bronwyn and Derek, and then to Molly and me. "So, all of this," he said, as he gestured towards Rowan, "is because of some teenage drama that occurred over the weekend?"

Before I could speak, Rowan answered. "Yes, Mr. Clendenin," she sniffed, and Molly and I exchanged glances. "I was with Derek Saturday, but he wasn't cheating on Bronwyn. I swear. I told him I'd seen Ainsley with an officer, a detective, from the Locklyn Police Department, but he didn't believe me until he saw her come out of the man's house. I thought it was a good idea to have a witness this time to catch them. The only reason Derek kissed me was to keep Ainsley from identifying him."

I shook my head as I clenched my hands into fists.

Rowan continued, "Ainsley hit me when she realized I know the truth about her and the cop and then she threatened Derek and me." The red-haired troublemaker sobbed.

I'd had enough. "Mr. Clendenin, Rowan's a vindictive liar."

"Ainsley, these accusations are serious. How old are you?" he asked.

"I'll be eighteen in less than two months. This whole thing is blown out of proportion. It's not what you think," I said as I stuck my tongue into the side of my cheek. I wanted to storm out of the office, out of the school.

"Ainsley's telling the truth, Mr. Clendenin," Molly piped up.

"I have pictures," Rowan suddenly offered, as she reached for her bag and produced her phone. The room got deathly quiet.

Mr. Clendenin put his hand up for me to stay silent.

Pictures? Pictures of what? I could easily explain this away if Mr. Clendenin would allow me to speak. There couldn't be anything on that phone other than me walking to Alec's truck.

Rowan handed her phone to the Vice-Principal, who studied the pictures as he scrolled through, then he made eye contact with me. "I'm going to forward these to my phone, but you have a lot of questions to answer, Ainsley."

~ ~ ~

Rowan's parents were the first to arrive. They glared at me as they shooed their daughter away. At this point, I didn't care. Mr. Clendenin hadn't declared it yet, but I guessed he would suspend me for hitting Rowan. I'd never been in trouble in school before, so this was new.

But the impending suspension didn't matter. Mr. Clendenin thought I was having an affair with the young detective. And worse, Rowan had pictures of something, although it couldn't be much. I'd seen her with her phone up as I was getting into the SUV. Neither Alec nor I had done anything to give the impression there was something more to us, something romantic.

But I was never supposed to be at Alec's house. Not the first time and not the second. He apparently hadn't told anyone I'd been there, although Kelsey had seen me the first time and knew without a shadow of doubt that I was there Saturday.

Molly patted me on my arm which pulled me from my thoughts. "Hey, it's going to be okay," she said. Molly sat in the hall outside of the office with me although Mr. Clendenin had ordered everyone back to class except for Rowan and me since no one else was involved in the physical altercation. Molly decided to stay with me until Mom came and the secretary didn't argue with her.

When Mom arrived, she was like a lost puppy, her wide eyes darting around the secretary's office. I couldn't tell if she wanted to ask me if I was all right or berate me for hitting Rowan. Mr. Clendenin had only told her over the phone about the fight as he didn't know the rest until after he'd called her.

Mr. Clendenin came out and ushered Mom into his office and shut the door. Molly patted my leg and then headed to class as I sunk further into the wooden bench.

This was going to be bad.

CHAPTER EIGHT

M r. Clendenin finally opened his office door. "Thank you, Stella for coming in. You'll keep me updated on the situation?"

"Of course, Nick. Thank you," she said, as she walked to the counter to sign me out.

She jerked her head for me to follow her. I grabbed my backpack and tried to keep up with her as she walked quickly to the car. Neither one of us spoke as we got in and Mom drove to the house and pulled into the driveway.

Then she exploded.

"You have one chance to explain to me what happened this morning, Ainsley. No more lies. Vice-Principal Clendenin showed me those pictures. Nick forwarded them to me. And to think I trusted Detective Graham." She turned the engine off and opened her door.

"Mom, I can explain."

"Oh, you are right about that. In the house. Now!"

I hadn't seen Mom this angry in a long time. She was on the verge of screaming, but it was coming out as a hiss because of the neighbors. I followed her straight into the house and up to the living room. Mom threw her purse and jacket onto the loveseat. The Michael Kors knock-off handbag bounced and landed on the floor, but Mom didn't care as she whirled around to face me.

"Well?"

"Okay. I went to Detective Graham's home Saturday morning to talk with him about the case. He was on his way to the station and offered to drop me off at Molly's. As I got into his truck, I saw Rowan Wesley kiss Derek Killian, Bronwyn's boyfriend. They saw me, too."

"Oh, I know that from the pictures." Mom tossed her phone at me and I barely caught it. "Go ahead. Take a look. Then try explaining this to me again."

I scrolled through the text messages from an unknown number, apparently Mr. Clendenin's number. The pictures had downloaded out of order. The images showed an undeniable Alec getting into the driver's seat, him helping me into the SUV with his hand on my lower back, us walking out of his house with me in the front and him wearing his ball cap, head down.

Then the zoomed-in kicker: a profile pic of Alec sitting on his bannister with his shirt off and drinking his coffee while I stood a few feet away, with an unbuttoned top button and a stupid grin planted on my face. The last picture was the shirtless Alec holding the glass door open for me as I walked inside his house, his eyes on me. Rowan must have stood on the other side of Alec's neighbor's house to get this shot.

Crap.

Rowan was a sneaky little…

"Are you having sex with that man, Ainsley?"

"What? No." I stared at her in disbelief. Of course, this was what she would believe with pictures of me at his home in secret.

"Mom, listen to me."

"Why should I? Lately you've been lying to me about where you're going. I should have seen this coming. He tried to hide it, but I caught the look he gave you when he saw you dressed for that exhibit. I noticed you've been dressing differently, more grown up. You've lost weight and ditched the junk food." She placed her hands on her hips as she turned to face the picture window.

I wasn't sure what to say. In the past week, I had started taking better care of myself, but it was more about valuing myself. Like Alec had suggested.

Mom turned back around. Her mouth opened as if I'd knocked the air out of her. "Did you even go to that art exhibit with Molly? Or, did you and Detective Graham go back to his place? Was that artwork yesterday a gift from him?"

"No, Mom. He took us to the exhibit. There's nothing going on between us other than the case. I promise you. I'm probably the last person he'd want to be with right now," I said, as I thought about Kelsey as she had hurled insults through the phone at me. "As for the artwork, that was probably from Declan or maybe Elijah. I'm still unclear on that. Declan called last night and asked me out on a date for Wednesday evening. Rowan is just jealous and spiteful."

Mom nodded her head. "I know she is, but you gave her plenty of ammo, didn't you? Now, we'll have to deal with her medical bills from her hospital visit and I can only hope her parents don't sue us."

She was quiet for a moment. "I went to school with Mr. Clendenin and he's not going to suspend you. He thinks you're lashing out and attaching yourself to Detective Graham because of your father's death."

I clasped my hands together and brought them to my mouth. This had nothing to do with Dad. "I don't have daddy issues," I said through gritted teeth, and tried to keep the sarcasm in my voice at an all-time low.

"Rowan told Mr. Clendenin that she's seen you at Detective Graham's house several times," she said quietly.

I took a deep breath. "That's not true, Mom. I've only been there twice."

"Twice!?" she practically screamed.

"I remembered something I thought was important about the surveillance video from the store that Detective Graham and Detective Tudor were going to watch. I went straight there that morning and told him. Mom, his girlfriend Kelsey was there. Other than not telling you, neither of us have done anything wrong."

Mom chewed on her bottom lip. I could tell she was torn between questioning everything I'd told her to wanting to believe her little girl was still intact. "Was his girlfriend there Saturday?"

"Well, no. Not that day."

"Then why did Rowan tell Mr. Clendenin you were in the house for over a half hour with the apparently shirtless detective?" She pointed at her phone still in my hands.

I glanced at the last pic of shirtless Alec as he let me into his home. Into his life.

"He was on his way to the station after breakfast. I stayed and ate while we talked about the case. Then he got dressed and we left."

Mom's eyes almost bulged out of her face as she shook her head. "I need to call the Chief of Police," she announced, as she reached for her phone.

"Mom, you can't. You'll get Alec fired over nothing."

"Alec?! You call him by his first name?" She grabbed the phone from my hands.

"Mom, please. He's my friend."

Mom was already calling the number stored in her phone from the night at the junior high. I walked slowly to the couch and sunk down into the cushion. Alec was going to lose his job over Rowan and Derek. Over me.

Mom left the living room and headed to the back deck when she finally connected to the Chief.

I couldn't breathe. If I tried to warn Alec, we'd look guiltier and it would put him under suspicion. I didn't think my age was really the factor as I was too close to eighteen for Alec to get into trouble. But, if they thought he'd crossed a line with a witness during an investigation that could lead to disciplinary action. I was sure of it.

I needed help. I needed help from someone who could see this objectively. I slipped over to the patio doors in time to hear Mom tell the Chief something about inappropriate behavior, possible suspicions, and teenage crushes.

I suddenly knew who I wanted to talk to about this dilemma. I grabbed my backpack and quietly crept out the front door before I sprinted full force back to the high school to see Ms. Maren Bell.

~ ~ ~

Although Ms. Bell's phone number and email address were on a sticky note in my bag, I wanted to confide in her in person. This was too much for a message. I waited near the school doors with my head down away from the camera until a parent came out with their student. I slipped in and quickly made my way to Ms. Bell's classroom as I prayed I wouldn't run into Mr. Clendenin.

I waited outside of her classroom and impatiently watched the clock as two minutes ticked by agonizingly slow. When the bell rang, I almost pulled the door off its hinges to get inside as students were gathering their things to move to their next class. Ms. Bell would have ten minutes before her next class period.

The teacher stood at her desk, signing a paper for a student.

"Ms. Bell? I need to speak with you, please," I pleaded in a rush of words.

Ms. Bell looked at me startled. She handed the student the paper and then nodded at me. "What is it, Ainsley? I heard you were in a fight this morning with another girl."

"Rowan Wesley. But that's only part of the reason I'm here. Someone I care about is in trouble and I don't know what to do. I don't know how to fix it."

"Okay. I need you to slow down and start from the beginning. Is this your friend you told me about before?"

"I think you and I both know I was talking about me."

She nodded. "Go on."

As if someone had lifted the gates and let the floodwaters pour out, I told Ms. Bell about seeing the creatures, the Muladach. I told her about finding the body at the old school and about Alec being the only one, besides Molly, who truly believed me. I told her about going to his home and about the horrible, horrible Rowan Wesley spying on me. I told her that even worse, my mother was on the phone with the Chief of Police and Alec would probably lose his job over something he didn't do because people thought we had a sexual relationship.

When I finished, I was nearly out of breath as I choked back tears.

Ms. Bell studied my face for a moment before she answered me. "I do believe you, Ainsley," she said, as she pulled me gently over to the windows and away from the incoming students.

"Sit in the back while I teach this class. I need to tell you something important that may answer some of your questions. It's about your father."

With that, Ms. Bell walked back to her desk and addressed the class about today's topic. The room spun as I slid into a chair in the back. My father? What did he have to do with any of this? Oh please, don't tell me the only person who might help me thinks I have issues stemming from Dad's death, too.

My phone vibrated. It was Mom. Since I was already in a world of trouble and continued to fall face first, I turned it off.

~ ~ ~

As soon as class let out for lunch, Ms. Bell grabbed her bag and I followed her out into the hall. "We're going to the school library. When your father was alive, did he ever say anything to you about demons?"

"My father? No, of course not. My mother is the horror writer."

"I know she is and she's very talented. But your father may have inadvertently given her some ideas."

"What are you talking about?" I asked, as I held the school library door open. The teacher motioned for me to follow her to the back. Apparently, the library was deserted during lunch.

Ms. Bell set her bag on a table, carefully pulled out a scroll and unrolled it across the wooden surface. "I've been carrying this with me ever since you came to me the first time about your "friend". Your father was a self-professed demonologist. He was highly regarded in the South with paranormal investigators and even with certain Roman Catholic priests and Jewish Rabbis who needed his help. He always insisted that it could never interfere with his family and the life he'd built with your mother. I'm pretty sure your mother doesn't know any of this," she said, as she lowered her eyes.

"Ms. Bell, I knew my father very well. He was home every night except when he had a business trip or…"

Ms. Bell cut me off. "Please, call me Maren. Your father didn't do his investigations all the time after you were born. Only select and dire cases, usually referred to him by a particular organization. This secret society specializes in demonic cases and is led by people of various denominations. Your father would call them business trips so as not to worry your mother."

I shook my head. "How do you know any of this?"

"I helped him a great deal on a few of these cases. I met him through one of the paranormal societies in West Virginia and he would ask me to attend to help confirm that the people he suspected being influenced by a demon did not in fact have some type of mental disorder."

I was stunned. My father had led a double life?

Maren continued, "Your father had a biblical gift called discernment of spirits. It made him an excellent demonologist because he saw and felt inhuman creatures – demons – in the area. It was dangerous work. His gift made him a beacon. If he saw a demon, chances were the demon could pick him out of an ocean of people. They were aware of his presence."

She slid the document over to me.

"I have a box of your father's things at my home if you'd like to come by tomorrow night, but this was a scroll he kept. It gives directions on how to expel a demon cluster."

"Demon cluster?"

"Sometimes demons work together, a few at a time. They may work together to influence an entire group of people or to endow one human with enough evil to do horrible things. Unspeakable things. From what you've told me about seeing the demons, what did you call them, Muladach? You saw the Muladach with a man, I assume the man is the killer the police are searching for. He will be hard to catch if the demons are influencing him, and others close to him, to throw off suspicion."

"What can I do?" I asked.

"Together we can possibly stop and send the demons away. I believe you have inherited your father's gift of discernment. The goal of the inhuman creatures is to thwart God's plans and destroy mankind. Although we can send the demons back to Hell, they will make their way back to this plane. Maybe not to the same human, but another. The other dangerous aspect of confronting this evil is the killer himself. Do the police have any idea who he is?"

"No, I don't think so. Although I haven't talked to Alec since Saturday morning." I hadn't told her about our brief conversation Sunday.

"Hmm. Let me give you my address and I want you to try to come over tomorrow evening, so I can give you your father's things. They may help you. But, please be careful. Serial killers sometimes like to get close to their victims. He may not be targeting you, but the demons are aware of your presence and have probably told him to watch for you. These types of killers enjoy cat and mouse games. They are curious and get a thrill from being in control. He may know who you are, but you won't know who he is until it's too late."

Maren rolled up the scroll and placed it carefully back in the bag.

"I'll try. I'm in so much trouble over Alec too. What should I do about that?"

Maren's mouth turned down as she shook her head. "There's not a whole lot you can do about that, I'm afraid. You claim nothing ever happened between you, but the evidence says differently. Allowing you into his home and asserting himself into your life like he has makes him look guilty. He's going to have to face the consequences of crossing that line with a witness in a case, a high school student. However, you maintain your innocence and dignity through all of this. You can tell your mother you came to see me at the school for an emergency counseling session. But, no more hitting little priss-face girls who are as crooked as a dog's hind leg. Trust me, if I can't hit Rowan Wesley, you shouldn't either."

~ ~ ~

The next morning, Molly picked me up for school. We'd barely pulled out onto the street when she asked how things went with Mom last night. I filled her in quickly with our conversation about Alec and Mom calling the Chief of Police.

"Yeah, Mom told me about whispers around the station that Detective Graham was pulled off The Artist Case," she paused as she stopped for the light in front of the school and gave me a sideways glance, "because of his involvement with you."

"The Artist Case?"

"Apparently, that's what the police dubbed those three murders. I heard Mom tell Dad that all the framed art are actually pieces of flesh, the victims' tattoos. Each one is extremely detailed and probably took a tattoo artist hours and hours to create. They are releasing the details to the media today."

"Like the one we saw from the woman. Why would someone do that?"

"I don't know. Because they're crazy. I heard the flesh and everything underneath was expertly removed. That's freaking scary."

"Maybe they're crazy and evil. And they pulled Alec off the case because of me." I pulled at a string on my ripped jeans.

"So, you saw Ms. Bell. What did she think?"

I gave Molly the Cliff Note version of Ms. Bell's advice about Alec but decided not to mention Dad or any of the demonologist stuff. I still wasn't entirely sure I wanted to believe something like that about my own father.

"After I got back home, Mom was furious at me since I'd left suddenly, but then she calmed down after I told her I'd seen Ms. Bell. Although, it was a bit embarrassing when Mom called her to confirm that I'd been there. She was afraid I'd taken off to Alec's house again. Whatever the Psych teacher told Mom about him caused her to approach the subject from a different perspective. Mom started talking about how when she was in high school, every emotion felt magnified a thousand times over."

"Ah, the parent-teen talk of when-I-was-your-age," Molly joked.

I laughed. "Kind of. She told me she could certainly see why Detective Graham and I would want to spend time together, but the timing is inappropriate."

"Hmmm," was all Molly replied, as we got out of her car and headed into the school.

The entire day was spent with whispers behind my back. Rowan's nose wasn't broken, and she was back at school, but steered clear of me. Derek also stayed away from me, although I saw him trying to talk to Bronwyn at her locker before lunch. A few people made jokes about me punching Rowan. Some made outright rude comments and gestures about me and "that cop."

I couldn't wait to start my receptionist job at the gym after school. I needed some mature conversation.

CHAPTER NINE

"You want me to wipe *butt sweat* off the machine seats?" I asked Henry.

The tall man laughed. "Yes. The members are supposed to wipe off the equipment when they're done, but at the end of the evening, I'd like for you to go back over each piece."

Henry and I were in his office going over the paperwork and my responsibilities for the position.

"I also need you to take the trash out to the dumpster around back, but there will always be someone here with you to lock up. Don't worry about that."

I nodded my head. I was pretty sure I could swing trash duty.

"Okay, last thing and then you can go home. Here's a short video about gym etiquette I need you to watch. Then you're free. I'll be up front. You can leave my phone on the desk when you're done," he said, as he handed me his cell. He shut the door behind him.

The video was about fifteen minutes long and covered everything about cleaning the machines before and after use to putting the weights back. I sure hoped people returned the heavy weights. There was no way I could possibly move some of them. Not unless I laid down on the floor and pushed them with my legs.

When the video finished, I set Henry's phone on his desk carefully and picked up my backpack. It seemed lighter today. Either I had less homework, or I hadn't paid attention in class for the assignments. It was a toss-up.

I shut Henry's office door behind me and started down the hall.

"Ainsley."

I jerked my head up at the sound of his voice. Alec stood in the break room with a water bottle in his hand. He must've just finished his workout as he was dressed in a pair of shorts, a gray muscle shirt, and his Nikes. He still had some sweat on his face and his arms were larger than usual. Was that the "pump" the guys at school talked about when they worked out?

I walked into the room and set my bag on a chair. I couldn't tell him, but I'd missed seeing him the past few days. I swallowed hard. I didn't know what to say.

"I'm sorry," we both said at once and then smiled.

"I'm sorry," I tried again. "I'm sorry I got you in trouble with the Chief and they pulled you off the case. I never should have shown up at your home, especially the second time. I knew that girl had seen me. She had pictures. I guess I'm trying to say that you didn't do anything wrong. It was all me."

Alec studied me a moment and then took a deep breath. "No, you're wrong about that. Ever since I met you, not even a week ago, I've believed incredible stories about demons, seen something I can't explain, lost my girlfriend, and been placed on a sixty-day suspension."

I made a face at his list, but he put up his hand for me to let him continue. "I almost crossed a line at the art exhibit and knew I was in dangerous territory. When you came to my house the first time, I should have sent you away. When you showed up Saturday, I should've told you to go home. But, I didn't. I didn't want to. When Kelsey saw your jacket, she exploded, but it didn't bother me that she left. It bothered me that I hadn't told her. That's on me."

We were both quiet for a moment. I didn't know what to say to that. What did he mean? Did he want me around?

"I didn't know they suspended you."

"Yeah. It could have been a lot worse," he said, as he took a drink of water. "It's only for sixty days because my service record is otherwise commendable. Then it's over. I decided to use this time to workout and hang with friends a little more. Congratulations on your new job, by the way. Henry told me you were here for orientation." He smiled and gave me that wink I hadn't seen for too long.

"Thank you. And thank you for putting in a good word for me," I said. "Um, does Henry know about this?" I asked, and waved my hand between us.

Alec made the same motion with his hand. "This?" he asked and laughed.

I nodded. "Truth be told, I don't want Henry to think I'm some sort of troublemaker."

"He's my friend. He doesn't think that way about you."

"I know you're off The Artist Case, but I did find out something yesterday," I said.

Alec's face took on a serious expression. "How did you know we call it The Artist Case?"

"So, it *is* true? All the bodies had their tattoos removed and the killer preserved and framed them?"

"If you know something, Ainsley, we need to tell David, Detective Tudor."

"It's about the demons. They surrounded me the other day in broad daylight, but this time I couldn't see them. That's why I called you Sunday. When everything blew up way out of proportion yesterday, I went to see the Psychology teacher at school. She's also a counselor. I went to ask for advice, but instead she told me the craziest story. She swears that my father was a demonologist brought in by an organization for serious demonic cases. She wants me to come by her house this evening. She has a box of Dad's things. Things that could expel the demons and maybe unmask the killer."

"You're not going to go by yourself, are you?" Alec asked, concern clearly visible.

"She's a teacher from school. I don't think she's a murderer. Plus, I didn't tell Molly about any of that, so I can't ask her to go."

Alec nodded his head. "I'll take you."

"I can't ask you to do that. You're already in trouble because of me," I said, as I watched Alec set his water bottle on the break room counter.

He crossed the narrow room until he was right in front of me and in one swift motion, cupped my face with his hands, like he did in the SUV at the art exhibit. Except this time, I wasn't going to ugly cry. Instead, I placed one hand on his arm and the other on his chest. His shirt was damp, but I could feel his heart pounding under my palm.

"Listen to me. Please," he whispered. "I know the timing is off with you turning eighteen very soon, but I want to go with you this evening. And after everything calms down, I was thinking maybe we could go out on a date in the future. *After* your birthday. If I can get your mother to agree."

The fire behind his green eyes sparked.

"What if Mom doesn't agree?" I asked.

Alec dropped his hands. "Then I'll have to respect her wishes and wait until after you graduate in the spring. Come on, I'll take you to this teacher's home. Let me run by my place first to change clothes and grab your jacket off the dining room table."

~ ~ ~

Although it was only a little after four-thirty, the sky grew dark. I found myself anxious as we parked the SUV in front of Alec's house. I peeked out the windows for Rowan, or maybe Derek, but I didn't see anyone. Most people were probably still at work.

Alec climbed out of the truck and opened my door. He didn't seem at all phased by the threat of a spying Rowan now. Maybe it was because the Department had already disciplined him with the suspension.

I waited in the living room while Alec quickly showered and dressed. When he emerged, he filled the room with a warm woodsy amber and soft citrus scent.

"What's wrong?" he asked.

"Nothing's wrong."

"You're blushing," he said and winked as he tossed me my black vest.

I wasn't sure why. Alec had thrown on a pair of jeans, Timberland boots, and a raglan tee. It wasn't like he was wrapped in a towel this time.

A knock on the door made me jump. Alec put his hand up for me to stay quiet.

"Who's there?"

"Alec, it's me, David," came the disembodied voice through the front door.

Alec moved in front of the door so that his body blocked the oval frosted glass. He motioned for me to go into the guest bedroom. I slipped past him and shut the bedroom door behind me but leaned against it. The bedroom was pitch dark now since he didn't keep a lamp on in this room. I certainly didn't want to bump into anything. Apparently, Alec didn't care about Rowan and her camera app but an unannounced visit from his partner was another matter.

I heard the front door open. "Hey, David, come on in."

"Hey man. What have you been doing?" I heard Detective Tudor's voice. I'd never thought about Alec and Detective Tudor being anything more than partners on the job, coworkers, but this seemed like a casual visit. I hoped it wouldn't take long so I could get to Ms. Bell's house before Mom started to worry. She probably figured I was still at orientation with Henry.

"I just got back from the gym and I'm headed out to meet a couple of friends. What's going on?"

"I'm still trying to figure out what happened, man. I knew there was something up when we went to that girl's house and she acted like she knew you. You didn't tell me you'd already met."

"I didn't know she was the witness until she came home." Alec suddenly sounded tired.

"Yeah, but to have her here? At your home?"

"Nothing happened. Yes, I should've handled that better. But I've taken the suspension and learned the lesson about befriending witnesses."

"Befriending witnesses. I don't think I've ever heard it stated quite like that before." Detective Tudor's voice took on a hard edge.

"Look, David, I should've told you about Ainsley coming over here. I didn't. But, she is an amazing young woman. I'm seriously considering asking her out in the future."

Detective Tudor let out a disgusted sound as my eyes welled up with tears. Alec was defending me from his partner, who apparently didn't like the idea.

"If you do, no one is going to believe the story that you weren't fooling around with her during this investigation. Plus, the strange anomaly on the videotape aside, she's probably imagined those creatures. She could be displaying signs of early mental illness. Think about it, man. She lost her father and you're probably the first father figure she's had in her life since then. I get it. She's young and pretty. Trust me. If she'd thrown herself at me that way, I'd seriously consider it, too. We've all been there, but this is your career. Better to walk away, Alec."

The living room got quiet.

"I have to get going. My friends are waiting on me." I strained to hear Alec's voice.

"All right." I heard the front door open. "Oh, I probably shouldn't tell you this, but we got a breakthrough in the case. The mat board the killer used is of a museum quality and not sold in very many stores. We narrowed it down to two places in Charlotte. One place is pulling the receipts. Hopefully, the suspect used a credit or debit card. The other is a museum and they're checking inventory."

"That's good to hear. Could the suspect have found the mat boards at a university?"

"I don't know, but that's a good idea. I'll look into it."

"Did we find out anymore about the tattoos on the victims?"

"Not much. I have the images from pictures family members sent in to us. Each tattoo was detailed in its artwork. We're not talking about a rose or an anchor or an I Love Mom tattoo. We're talking about scenes from story books. Princesses riding on stallions in front of medieval castles. Warriors burying their dead in Celtic cemeteries. I'll text you the images. Crazy stuff. As for your frame theory, we're still looking into it."

"Good. Before I left the station, Nikki Hiroto stopped me. She picked up traces of a second individual at the scene. Looks like our guy *is* working with an accomplice."

"Yeah, that's what she told me too."

"I hope we nail these guys before they kill someone else."

"Me too, man. Me too."

The men said goodbye and I heard Alec shut the front door and turn the deadbolt. I felt the doorknob turn in my hand as he pushed the door open.

"Hey, are you still in here?" he asked quietly, clearly amused at me as I stood in the dark.

His silhouette took on a shadow-man effect backlit from the living room, but I could still make out his features.

"We need to wait a few minutes before we leave. I want to make sure David's gone."

"I heard Detective Tudor. He's probably right. For your career, it might be best if you walked away after this case. You've worked too hard to lose it all – over being my friend," I whispered the words, as the lump in my throat wouldn't let me speak otherwise.

Alec stepped further into the room and pulled me into a hug. It was the first time he'd hugged me, and I forced back the tears and relaxed in his strong arms. For the first time in a long time, I felt safe. Safe from the demons and killers, safe from conniving girls and rumors, safe from well-meaning adults.

"David is concerned, but he's not right. Not about you." He pulled back and playfully pulled at a lock of my hair that had wrapped around his hand. "Come on, let's go see this teacher."

~ ~ ~

Maren Bell lived in a two-story brick townhouse not far from Bronwyn's property near the outskirts of Locklyn. She answered her front door only seconds after I'd pressed the doorbell.

"Ainsley! I'm so happy you came. And you brought a friend," she observed, as her voice changed from excited to Southern Appalachian smooth.

"I hope that's okay," I said. "This is Detective Alec Graham."

"Oh, yes. Of course." Her eyes flitted over Alec.

Either he didn't seem to notice, or didn't care, as he held his hand out to shake hers.

"I'm Maren Bell. I teach Psychology at the high school. Ainsley is in my class," she said, as she shook his hand and smiled. I'd never seen her smile like that before even in class. It was a playful smile. Maybe it was just me, but why did it seem like my teacher was flirting with my sort-of-possible-future-boyfriend?

I hadn't recovered from Maren's strange behavior when Alec slipped his arm around my waist and pulled me closer to him. "You told Ainsley you have some information about her father? Some of his belongings?"

Maren's smile diminished as she observed Alec's hand resting on my hip. "Yes, I do. You probably have a lot of questions. Come with me."

We followed her into the dining area of her home where a large oak table was loaded down with binders and books. On one end was a banker's box. It was labeled *Gerry* in a feminine scrawl.

Maren tapped the lid with her polished nail. "These were the things your father kept for his work."

"The box says Gerry," I said quietly. "No one called my father that. Not even my mother. She stills calls him Gerald."

Maren lowered her eyes but remained silent. Something pricked at me as I stared at the teacher who dressed like she was in her twenties with her gorgeous highlighted hair, eyelash extensions, and manicured nails.

Don't go there, Ainsley. You're reading too much into this. It's a stupid banker's box.

I removed the lid and started pulling things out of the box. A purple sash with gold embroidery, a heavy brass cross with a red stone in the center, tons of papers, a couple of books, a large leather bound Bible and a smaller version, and a large binder. I pulled his passport out of the box and opened it. Italy, Ireland, Spain, Israel.

How could he have traveled out of the country, off the continent, and never told us?

There was only one thing left in the bottom of the box. As my hand wrapped around it, I knew at once what it was. I held it up to my face and watched as the light from Maren's small chandelier bounced off the silver pendant. The silver pendant with the horse and two riders on one side and my father's initials on the other.

The silver pendant he never took off. The one lost in the accident.

I turned on Maren who stood perfectly still in the doorway to the kitchen. "Where did you get this?" I growled.

"Your father was on a business trip regarding a demon possession. The accident happened on his way back. Somehow the organization was told about the accident and they asked me to go to the hospital and remove anything that might indicate what Gerry was doing before the wreck."

"*This* doesn't indicate anything about demons," I said, as I slung the pendant around by its chain. "This was his. He never took it off. When did you take this?"

"I arrived at the hospital moments before you and your mother. I passed you in the hall, but you didn't notice me."

"But why did you take it?" I asked, as my voice cracked.

Maren's eyes filled with tears as she leaned against the doorway. "Because he never took it off. Because it was the only thing left of him. We didn't have an affair. He loved your mother too much," she sniffed. "But I cared a great deal for him." Defeated, she slid down the wall to the floor. She pulled her knees into her chest and cried.

I held the pendant in my palm and flipped it over. It read *GVR*. I turned to Alec. "This was my dad's pendant. He wore it every day of his life. When they brought him into the hospital, they said they thought it must've been lost in the accident," I told him, as Alec reached around and rubbed my back.

"He used to tell me it protected him from evil, especially while travelling. It was just something he believed. His initials are engraved on this side. GVR."

"Those aren't his initials," Maren said, as she slowly rose from the floor, gaining her composure.

"Yes, they are," I said. "Gerald Victor Reynolds. GVR."

Maren shook her head. "It's GVR for *gaza virtute et robore*. It's Latin for the Wealth of Power and Strength."

I ran my finger over the letters. Was Maren right? "He told me these were his initials."

Maren hesitantly stepped closer to me. "They were also his initials, yes. His destiny. He was chosen for his gift of the discernment of spirits and his ability to expel demons with great power and strength. This helped to protect him during many demonic battles. He didn't lie to you."

"He didn't tell me the whole truth," I said. "It's getting late. I have to go home. Can I keep this box here until I figure something out?"

"Of course," Maren agreed. Then she glanced between Alec and me. "It might be a better idea if I take you home though. I spoke with your mother yesterday and seemed to calm her down about this," she said as she wagged her finger at us. "But she probably won't take too kindly to him bringing you home tonight."

"She's right," Alec said. "She should be the one to drive you home and meet your mother."

I nodded in agreement.

We waited outside at Alec's SUV while Maren pulled herself together to meet Mom in person. I wasn't sure that's what she'd meant by driving me home, but Alec seemed to think it was a good idea.

Alec leaned against the truck. "Do you believe her?"

"Yes, I think so. I think she sometimes helped Dad on his investigations and, eventually, she fell in love with him. But you heard her. He loved my mom too much to cheat," I answered.

Alec nodded.

"You're the detective. Do you think she's telling the truth?"

He took a deep breath as he narrowed his eyes at Maren's townhome. "Yeah. The way she behaved about that necklace, I'd say she's telling the truth."

I pulled Dad's chain out of my pocket as I walked over to him. He appeared surprised as I purposefully leaned into him. He placed his hands on my waist and inhaled sharply.

"Hold still," I whispered. I unclasped the chain and wrapped it around his neck. I could barely clasp it back because I was keenly aware of the rise and fall of Alec's chest against mine. With it finally latched, I stared up into his eyes. "He wore this for protection and it worked, according to Maren. I need to know that you're safe."

He studied my face as he leaned closer to my lips. "Thank you," he whispered.

"We should get going, kids." Maren Bell's voice rang out from behind me.

Alec and I both sighed.

~ ~ ~

I opened the front door with my key, but then knocked loudly before starting up the steps to the living room. I hadn't called Mom and told her I was bringing someone home.

"Mom?" I yelled. Maren followed me inside.

"Ainsley? Did you stay over?" Mom's voice called over the bannister.

"Mom, I want you to meet someone," I said.

Mom came over to the top of the steps with Ben on her heels. Her eyes widened, but then her face relaxed into a smile.

"Mom, this is Ms. Maren Bell from the school. You talked to her yesterday."

"Why, yes. Come on up and have a seat. Would you like some coffee or tea?" Mom asked, as she waved her hand at the loveseat. Ben hopped over onto the couch and I slid down beside him. I hadn't seen much of him all week.

Maren sat rigidly down on the cushion. "Oh no, thank you. I can't stay long. I happened to be driving by and saw Ainsley walking home from the gym."

"Well, that's nice. Thank you for taking the time to talk with me yesterday," Mom said.

"You're welcome. I work as a part-time counselor when I'm not teaching, so it's second nature to help. And Ainsley is always welcome."

"Thank you," Mom said, as she eyed me. "It probably wouldn't be a bad idea if Ainsley could sit in for a couple of counseling sessions with you. Things have been difficult since Gerald passed away two years ago," she pointed at a portrait on the wall. It was one of Mom and Dad taken a few years prior to his death.

I narrowed my eyes as I watched Maren follow Mom's gaze to the picture. I wasn't sure if Maren had any pictures of Dad, but from the expression on her face, I'd guess not. The teacher smiled a bittersweet smile.

"Of course, I have no problem helping your daughter through this confusing time. I'm sure her father would've wanted it that way."

The two women agreed that I would attend a couple of sessions with the teacher. My opinion was apparently not needed. After Maren left, I started for my room.

"Hey, how was orientation?" Mom asked.

"It was good. I have to do lots of cleaning before closing time though, but it's no big deal."

"Okay, well, there is pizza on the counter if you want some." I walked into the kitchen, but the thought of pizza didn't sound good, so I decided on a cold protein shake from the refrigerator. As I passed Mom on my way to the hall, she sniffed the air.

"You must've started cleaning for them a little early," she said and laughed. "I smell a citrusy, woodsy scent."

"Yeah," I said, as I sniffed my shirt, "I have to clean sweat off the machines with that spray bottle."

I hurried to my room with Alec's scent on my shirt.

CHAPTER TEN

At five-thirty Wednesday morning, the landline rang three times before I assumed Mom answered. My alarm was set to go off in ten minutes anyway, so I switched it off and went to Mom's bedroom door. I opened it carefully in time to see her press the button on the phone and toss it on the bed.

"Who was that?"

"The school district. Your school cancelled classes today due to a break in the main water line."

"WooHoo. That's what I'm talking about," I exclaimed, as I shut her door and danced my way down the hall towards the kitchen. After the last few days at school, I needed a break.

I made myself a large cup of coffee and opened the pantry door. I was hungry this morning.

"Give me a minute, I'll make some scrambled eggs," Mom offered, as she headed for the Keurig.

"What time do you have to get Ben up for school?"

"Not for another hour and then I usually head out to the gym. Do you want to go this morning since you work out for free?" she asked.

"Umm, yeah. That could be fun."

"Don't you have that date with the artist this evening? Declan?"

I'd forgotten all about Declan since Alec had blown me away with the news that he wanted us to go out in the future.

"Yes, I'd actually forgotten about it," I admitted and laughed. "Forgetting a date. That's new."

"It'll do you good to get out and meet some other boys with different goals."

"Mom, what do you mean?" I asked in a dead-pan tone as I eyed her over the top of my coffee mug.

"Look, Ms. Bell has helped me to understand that you and Detective Graham do have feelings for one another, but she believes that you've both shown great restraint, although the timing is poor. I think keeping your options open is a smart idea. You said Declan goes to Queens and is very well thought of in the artistic circles there, right?" she asked, as she gathered the eggs from the refrigerator.

"He is," I said, "according to Elijah, Molly's friend. He's nice and I plan to keep my date with him this evening. But Mom, I would like for you to consider the fact that maybe Detective Graham – Alec – and I may want to date after I turn eighteen." I held my breath as she turned slowly from the stove to face me.

"I see."

The silence filled the kitchen.

"Here, finish stirring this. I'm going to see if your brother wants some before he gets ready for school."

Apparently, our conversation about my future with Alec was on pause.

~ ~ ~

After breakfast, I cleaned the kitchen while Mom helped Ben get ready for school and then I showered and dressed for the gym. It seemed silly to shower *before* the gym, but I didn't want to go feeling scuzzy. It'd been a long time since I'd wanted to work out, but I decided since I could do it now for free, why not?

Mom was the same way and she wasn't ready for at least an hour after Ben left. I waited on the couch and text Molly that I had a date with Declan this evening and no idea what to wear. I also sent her the pic of his artwork. It was hard keeping the details about Alec and Dad and Ms. Bell away from Molly, but she didn't need to be caught in the middle.

"Ready? Let's go," Mom said. I followed her down the stairs but stopped at the entrance to the family room.

"Mom, why don't we ever use the family room anymore?"

Mom paused at the garage door and turned around. "I don't know. It was your dad's favorite room to hang out in when he was off work. There are lots of memories in there. I guess I'm not ready to take those on."

I turned to face my mother with her blonde pineapple bun and minimalist makeup. "He loved you. You know that? A love that nothing, or *no one*, could separate. That's what I want someday. I want to know that the love of my life saw me for me. Not just the outside, but all of me, the deepest, darkest parts of me, and *only* me. And loved it all."

Mom smiled as she walked over to stand in front of me. She reached out her hand and pushed some stray hair away from my face. "And you'll have that one day, Ainsley. I don't doubt it one bit."

We drove to the gym and Mom parked the car, but before we got out, I spotted Alec's black SUV on the lot. He was here early now that he had more time on his hands. This could get ugly.

I turned, but Mom was already out of the car. I jumped out quickly and almost landed on my face on the blacktop. "Hey, Mom?"

She stood at the trunk. "What? Don't tell me you're backing out of our sweat sesh now."

What? Sweat sesh? Who was this woman? "No, Mom. That's not it. Before you go in, you need to know that Alec is here. That's his truck," I added and nodded in the general direction of the SUV.

"I see," she said, as she turned on her heel towards the gym.

"Mom." I skipped behind her. "Mom, please, I work here now. He and the owner are close friends. Please don't get me fired." Mom frowned at me as she jerked the gym door open. I followed her in like a wounded cat.

With one glance around the room, I spotted Alec right away. He laid on a weight bench with two heavy dumbbells, in the middle of a set of chest flys. He was focused on the ceiling.

But I wasn't the only one who spotted him. Mom made a beeline straight for the detective with me on her heel.

"Detective Graham," Mom's voice seethed, and Alec looked up at her startled. No amount of weights could defend him from Stella Reynolds.

He carefully set the dumbbells on the floor as he glanced from Mom to me and back again. He slowly stood up, towering over her by more than a half a foot, but Mom didn't move.

"Mrs. Reynolds, I-" Alec started, but Mom put her hand up.

"I wanted to personally tell you how disappointed I am in your inappropriate behavior where Ainsley is concerned."

Alec lowered his gaze. There was no use arguing with my mother.

Mom put her hands on her hips. "It's come to my attention however that you might have feelings for her. Is that true?"

Alec made eye contact with me before he attempted to look at Mom.

I held my breath.

"Yes, Ma'am. If it is alright with you, I'd like to take Ainsley out on a real date after the investigation is closed. Of course, after her birthday."

"Hmm," Mom said, as she nodded, but it was more of a 'is-that-right?' kind of nod than a nod of approval. "I know my daughter, and because I know her, I'm going to allow her to date you after December. However, you should know I've already told her to keep her options open. Eighteen is too young to get swept up in a serious relationship. As a matter of fact, you should know she has a date this evening with a boy from Queens University."

At that moment, I may have had an outer body experience. Why would she tell him that? Of course, Alec didn't know about my date. Even I'd forgotten about it.

Alec's green eyes flickered over to me. "I wasn't aware of that," he said slowly.

"Declan O'Hara asked me out after I received a gift from either him or Elijah. I'm not sure which one. Anyway, I'd forgotten about it until this morning," I added too quickly.

Alec nodded his head but remained silent.

"Well, now that we have that out of the way, in the future you may call me Stella. Since my daughter already calls you Alec, then I'm going to assume I can..." Mom's voice trailed off. Her eyes were locked on Alec's neck.

He was wearing Dad's medallion.

"Where did you get that?" Mom whispered.

Alec's face softened as he watched Mom's posture relax. "A friend gave it to me. It's supposed to protect the wearer from harm."

"My husband, Ainsley's father, had one like it. He wore his every day up until the day he died."

Mom turned slowly away from Alec and I followed her over to the elliptical machines.

"Thank you, Mom."

"For what?"

"For giving Alec and me your blessing."

"Well, technically, you are considered an adult. I don't want to see you jump the gun. Your father and I married at eighteen, but there isn't a man left on this planet like him," she said as she glanced over at Alec who was back to his weight set. "You know what? I really don't feel like working out this morning after all. Let's go grab a bite to eat."

"Sure, Mom. That sounds good." At the sound of the gym door opening, Alec mouthed the word, "sorry." I gave him a small smile as we left.

~ ~ ~

When Mom pulled the car into the garage, my phone rang. It was Declan.

"I heard your school is closed today because of the plumbing," he said, in his thick British accent.

"Yes, a water main broke. Are we still on for this evening?" I asked, as we got out of the car. I kind of hoped he'd changed his mind about our date. Mom motioned to me that she was headed upstairs, but I stayed on the lower level.

"Of course. Actually, I wanted to see if we could move it up earlier in the day. I could pick you up around noon. What do you say?"

"That would probably be better. Is there a certain dress code? You haven't told me where we're going."

"You wear whatever you want, and I'll find an activity that matches you."

After I hung up, I wandered through the family room with its brick fireplace and family portraits on the walls. Maybe if I started using the room again, Mom would eventually heal. When she'd seen the medallion on Alec, I could tell that it summoned the painful reminder Dad was gone. I prayed she would never discover that the one Alec wore *was* Dad's.

My phone vibrated in my hand.

"Alec?"

"Hi. I'm sorry if I made your mother uncomfortable. I would have left."

"You didn't make her uncomfortable. I think seeing the pendant threw her for a loop. She still grieves over Dad."

"So, you have a date with Declan O'Hara."

"Yes, today at noon. He called me Sunday after I received a gift delivered by FedEx. If it was from him, then I know he paid a small fortune in shipping. He denies sending it, but I don't think it's from Elijah. He's too into Molly. Declan called moments after I spoke with you, but that's when Kelsey was there."

"Oh," he was quiet for a moment. "What did he send?"

"Hold on and I'll text you a pic." I maneuvered my phone until I could text the picture of the framed artwork to Alec. "I sent it."

"I'm a little nervous about you going out with O'Hara," he said.

"Why? Is this a jealousy thing?" I asked.

"No. I don't like the vibe I get from him. Call it investigative gut."

I sat down on the brick hearth and pulled my legs up. "Well, I think having you chaperone would qualify as not a real date." I laughed, but Alec didn't.

"I want you to be careful. You're not to tell this to anyone, including Molly and Elijah, but the police are investigating Declan quietly because the framed tattoos found near the victims were created by a professional. And those frames are all handcrafted with details similar to O'Hara's work. According to Nikki Hiroto, a particular vapor barrier was used on the frames to protect the integrity of the skin from the wood and from humidity changes."

"Oh."

"You know what? I have a better idea. After your date with O'Hara, why don't you meet me back at the gym? I'm going to take you to the gun range. You need to know how to protect yourself."

"Alec, we don't even own a gun," I said, a little shocked. And a little excited.

"That's okay. You can use mine today."

"Okay. Let's do it."

~ ~ ~

Since I planned to meet Alec to go to the gun range after my date with Declan, I decided to wear a pair of black jeans with my black boots and a rose gold sweater with shoulder cut-outs. I only hoped it wasn't too chilly today. Maybe I would bring my beige leather jacket just in case.

As I applied my makeup, I felt guilty about Declan. I was more excited about the gun range with Alec than giving Declan a chance and that didn't seem right. I braided my hair and added a short gold necklace as I stood in front of the piece of art. The one entitled *Ainsley*. The man felt very strongly about displaying his art in museums and yet, he may have sent me this work that was absolutely a masterpiece. Perhaps he was too shy to admit it was from him.

Declan arrived in a silver car right at noon. I opened the front door but waved for him to come upstairs to meet Mom in the living room. There was no way she was going to let me go without meeting the artist who'd named his work after me.

To be fair, not only had I forgotten our date until this morning, but I'd also forgotten how handsome and rugged the college senior was with his dark hair, mustache and beard. Today he wore a pair of jeans and an untucked dark blue dress shirt tailored to him. Declan was built, that was for sure. As soon as he greeted Mom with his accent, she almost swooned.

"Please, sit down, Declan. Ainsley tells me the work you displayed at the Art Exhibit was breathtaking. I know the piece you sent her is exquisite."

"Thank you, Mrs. Reynolds. You're too kind, but as much as I wish the gift was from me, it's not. Elijah Moore and I collaborate at times, so it may be from him. I'm working on what I consider to be my career masterpiece right now. I've crafted the frame and I only need to tack the piece onto its backing for it to be show-ready. I'm hoping to have the last piece ready tomorrow night. It's going to be the largest of the entire collection."

"You're awfully young to consider a piece as your career masterpiece," Mom observed and smiled.

"My career up until now, I suppose," Declan said, as his eyes scanned the room.

"It's in my room," I answered him before he asked the question. "I thought it was from you and I remembered you didn't want your work hanging in people's living rooms, so I hung it in my room where I could see it every morning."

"That's right, you did say that. Would it be possible for me to see it?"

I glanced at Mom. After everything with Alec, I wasn't sure if Mom would allow Declan near my bedroom.

"Of course," Mom said.

The three of us walked to my bedroom and I was thankful that I kept it neat most days. Especially today. "Here it is," I said, as I stood in front of the dresser.

Declan stared at the piece in awe. He ran his hands over the frame as he moved in closer to see the picture. "May I?" he asked.

I nodded as he removed the artwork from the wall and carefully flipped it over. He touched the plaque with the tip of his finger before looking up at me. "This *is* an exquisite piece. Would it be possible for me to borrow it for a few days? I'd like to remove the back and see what the artist used as canvas. There is something odd, yet strangely beautiful, about it."

"Well, I guess that would be fine. I honestly don't think Elijah would send me such an expensive gift while he's dating Molly. That doesn't make sense."

Declan's eyes glazed over as he held the frame close to his chest as if mulling something over.

"So, where are you two off to today?" Mom asked, as she must have also sensed the awkward moment.

Declan turned toward me and observed my outfit. "I'm thinking a movie and a late lunch. What do you say?"

"Sounds great, but we should get a move on. Since there was no school today, I told Henry he could call me in to work if they need me," I lied, as we moved into the hall. Although Mom had agreed that I could date Alec after December, it didn't mean she would allow me to hang out with him at a gun range.

"Oh, I didn't know that," Mom said. "Let me know if you go to work, so I'll know where you are."

I nodded my head as we said goodbye to Mom.

~ ~ ~

I chose a scary movie at the theaters, although Declan suggested a rom-com. I didn't know how I would feel about watching a romantic comedy with a guy who wasn't the one I had my eye on. Afterwards, we went to an expensive Mexican restaurant.

"I like this place, but I hardly ever get to come," I said, after we'd ordered our food.

"I had Elijah ask Molly what some of your favorite restaurants are. It was much easier than guessing," he smiled.

"Molly did very well then."

"Honestly, when I called you Sunday, I was afraid you'd turn me down and tell me you were involved with that detective. The one at the exhibit." He crossed his arms on the table as he leaned forward.

I wasn't sure what to say. "Detective Graham and I aren't involved like that, but we've become very close friends."

Declan nodded. "Hmm. But you like him?"

I took a sip of my iced tea. "Declan, I'm sure you didn't ask me out to talk about Detective Graham," I said and smiled. Hopefully, he would get the hint that this was a borderline awkward conversation.

"I don't want to see you get hurt. I see a lot of older guys at the school who go out with the freshman girls until they're done with them. Then it's over and the guy moves on, but the girl is pretty shaken up about it."

"You don't know Detective Graham. He's not like that," I said quietly.

"I'm sure he's not. I just feel compelled to warn you that there are guys like that in the world. Charmers."

"And are you one of those guys? A charmer?" I asked.

Declan took a drink of his soda and then winked. "Ah-ha. You think I'm charming. I knew it," he said.

I couldn't help but laugh. Although his warnings over Alec were unfounded, Declan was funny and charming. We spent the next half hour eating nachos and fajitas and talking about Declan's life in England until my phone vibrated on the table.

It was a text from Alec: **I'm at the gym. When you're ready, that is.**

"Is it him?" Declan asked.

"Who?" I asked startled.

"Your boss wanting you to work?"

"Yes. Yes, it is. Do you think you could drop me off at the gym?"

~ ~ ~

"Well, I guess I should be jealous now. You look gorgeous," Alec said, as I walked into the break room at The Locklyn Gym.

"Why, thank you, sir."

Alec grabbed two bottles of water out of the refrigerator Henry kept stocked for employees…and apparently his best friend. As he handed me one, I couldn't help but notice that although Declan was larger than Alec, Alec could hold his own. Although he wore a black and white raglan shirt, I could still picture him shirtless on Saturday morning.

"Did you have a nice date?"

I laughed. "Wow. You said that so nonchalantly. The date was nice. We saw a movie and ate at the Mexican restaurant in town."

"Oh, I see."

"Yep, and Declan is pretty hilarious."

"Well then, you'd better watch out. I might date him myself," Alec said, as he rolled his eyes.

I stepped a little closer to him. "But…I'm here with you now. I'm ready to go with *you*."

Alec studied my face intently and for a wonderful second, I thought he might kiss me. Instead, he smiled and took my hand. "Good. Come on. I can't wait to show you the range."

As we walked out of the gym, Alec's phone beeped, and he glanced down at it. He slowed his pace in the parking lot as he scrolled. Finally, he stopped beside the truck with a frown on his face.

"What's wrong?"

"Nothing really," he said slowly. "David, Detective Tudor, sent me the pictures of the victims' tattoos in the frames. He's supposed to send a pic of the back tattoo from the girl, the tattoo that we haven't found yet. Her family sent him a picture from when she was still alive from her Facebook. The killer may have kept it as a souvenir." He shook his head. "David was right. On the crime scene, it was almost impossible to study the details because of the chaos of the murders, but these are hauntingly beautiful. This killer is psychotic."

"I thought you were off the case," I said, as he opened the door.

"I am, but David's my partner. He's still going to send them to me. He wants my input. Plus, these are reminiscent of anthropodermic bibliopegy."

"What?" I asked.

"Haven't you ever heard of skin books? Book covers made from human skin?"

"No. Is that really a thing?"

Alec nodded.

"Why? Why is that a thing?" I asked, as my stomach slightly turned.

"Relax. It's not something practiced today. Well, not up until The Artist appeared. Sometimes, if a person was believed to be the personification of evil, once they died, someone would remove their skin and preserve it with oils through a tanning process. Then they would create a book from the skin, like a leather cover, and add in the details with gold lettering."

"Just like with the pieces left behind by The Artist."

"Pretty much. Nikki Hiroto said the PMF test labeled the proteins from the "canvas" as human, but the killer is using a process that dries and preserves the skin faster than allowing it to air dry somewhere." Alec shook his head again. "I can't believe you didn't learn about this in school."

"What school is going to randomly tell their students about skin books?"

He laughed at my serious question as he motioned for me to climb into the truck. "There are several still in existence today. I think a medical library in Philadelphia has a few."

"Can I see the pictures of the tattoos?" I asked, when I'd hoisted myself onto the leather seat.

"No. I promised David I wouldn't share them with you," he said, as he walked around and got in the driver's side.

"I was in your guest bedroom while he was there, and you never said that," I fussed and crossed my arms.

"He text me. Come on, buckle up. I can't go to the gun range the officers normally use because of the suspension, so we're going to a public one outside of town," he answered, as he motioned for me to hurry up and buckle my seatbelt.

"Let me see the pictures and I will."

Alec stared at me as if he couldn't believe I had the gall to argue with him over something as trivial as pictures. He might as well get used to my obstinate behavior. He turned in his seat and leaned over for the seat belt buckle hanging near my shoulder. "Or, I could do it myself," he whispered. He slowly pulled the belt across me and snapped it into place as his lips formed a little smirk, like he'd won this round.

Without much thought, I touched his cheek and ran my thumb over the stubble that I'd fallen hard over.

Then I kissed him.

As I did, I breathed him in. That warm woodsy scent that made the world stop spinning on its axis.

Alec ran his hand up my arm and around my neck as he kissed me back. There was a passion and an urgency behind it. After a long moment, he pulled back, and placed his forehead against mine.

"Ainsley, we can't do this right now. Not yet," he whispered breathlessly. He turned around and started the engine.

"It was just a harmless kiss," I said quietly.

He looked at me, his green eyes on fire. "With you, it will never be *just* a harmless kiss."

~ ~ ~

"Do you feel somewhat confident in my ability to protect myself now?" I asked, as Alec observed the bullet holes in the target a few hours later.

"I do for a target that's not moving. Unfortunately, most threats move towards you."

I leaned in a little closer to him. "What do you suggest?"

Alec smiled before he met my gaze. "There you go again, standing too close."

"Does it bother you?"

"It's important for me to take things slow with you. I've screwed up relationships in the past from moving too fast too soon. I don't want it to be that way with you. It *can't* be that way with you."

I nodded. "Fine. I'll try to not stand too close to you," I said, as I grinned and took another step closer.

"You really are driving me crazy," he whispered, as he loaded his gun again and set a new target.

"But in a good way, right?" I asked loudly, as he put his earmuffs on.

"You don't have to do that to get my attention. You've had it from Day One," he yelled, before he shot a round.

I scurried to put my earmuffs on. As I watched him shoot his gun with such control and focus, I couldn't help but smile to myself. From Day One. All along I'd thought I'd fallen hard over Alec, and that maybe it was a teenage crush. But, Alec had fought hard to keep his feelings for me private. He'd struggled not to cross that line.

Not long from now there wouldn't be a line anymore.

~ ~ ~

As we checked out from the gun range, Alec's phone beeped.

"Is it Detective Tudor again?" I asked.

"Yeah." He scrolled on his phone as we walked outside, but stopped short as soon as we stepped onto the parking lot. "Ainsley, where's that artwork Declan sent you?"

"He said he didn't send it to me. It's not his piece."

Alec stared hard at his phone, his jaw clenched. "But where *is* it?"

"Declan has it. It was hanging in my bedroom. Declan asked if he could see it and when I showed it to him, he seemed enthralled over it. He asked if he could borrow it for a few days. He plans to remove the backing and see what material the artist used."

Alec's eyes grew wide with alarm. "Come on. We need to go. I have to find David and tell him about this." He rushed me to the truck and as we got in, he handed me his phone.

I read the text message from David Tudor: **Here's the image of the female victim's tattoo. As you can see it's eerie. No wonder the killer would want to keep it. What do you think?**

I covered my mouth as I gasped. The picture was the back view of a woman in a bikini, the woman from the grocery store. Her back tattoo was of a Lady sitting by a pond. I swallowed hard as I zoomed in.

It was the same as the artwork I'd received.

"The killer sent *me* the framed tattoo?" I asked. I hadn't noticed we were already driving at a breakneck speed towards the town.

Alec's face registered both anger and worry, if that was possible. "Can you spend the night at Molly's tonight? I don't think you should go home."

"What about Mom and Ben?"

"They're not the target," he answered.

"Why would he target me? I don't have any tattoos," I said, as I text Molly.

"Maren told us the demons knew your father because he could see them. It's probably the same with you. You're the beacon now. You're a liability," he said the words with absolutely no emotion. *This* was Detective Graham on duty. Suspension or not.

My phone vibrated. "Molly text back that's fine. I'll need to call Mom as soon as I get there. Should I call Declan? What if the killer knows he has the artwork? He might do something horrible to Declan to keep him from discovering the truth of what it is."

"I'll handle O'Hara. I want you to stay as far away from him as possible right now." He glanced at me as his face softened a bit. "Please. And Elijah ,too. Until I can get with David to clear them both."

The wheels on the SUV squealed as he turned onto Molly's street. I grabbed the Oh Crap bar above my head. "You will call me and let me know what is happening, right?" I asked, as I fought to keep the tears at bay. Alec's serious reaction to Detective Tudor's text scared me.

He stopped in front of Molly's and got out. He surveyed the neighborhood before he opened my door. "Yes, I'll keep you informed. Stay with Molly and you'll be safe," he said, as I climbed out and stood on the sidewalk. Molly opened the front door.

"I feel safe with you," I whispered.

Although I could tell Alec was in a hurry and was already pulling up David's number on his phone, he stopped. He pulled me close and placed his forehead against mine as he cupped the side of my face in his hand.

"I promise you. I'm not going to let anyone hurt you," he whispered, and then brushed his lips against my forehead before he turned and walked around the SUV.

I stood on the sidewalk as he pulled away from the curb, the sound of a ringing phone filled the air as he placed his call through the truck's speakerphone.

I suddenly felt Molly's arm wrap around my shoulders. "I thought you were on a date with Declan. You okay?"

"I have a lot to tell you, Mol," I answered, as I stared at the back of Alec's truck as he drove to the end of the street.

"Let's go inside. I'll make us some hot cocoa and you can tell me when *this* started," she said, as she gestured towards the now-empty curb.

"That's not even the headline tonight."

~ ~ ~

While Molly made us a cup of hot cocoa, I called Mom and told her I was going to spend the night at Molly's and ride with her to school in the morning since the water main was repaired. Mom asked to speak with Mrs. Hiroto. My guess was to confirm my story was true which made me feel about an inch tall. Mrs. Hiroto was watching a movie in the family room, but she told Mom she didn't have a problem with me spending the night.

"Okay. Well, I'll feel better if you make sure you come straight home after school tomorrow," Mom ordered.

"Of course. I will," I promised her, with no intention of breaking that promise. After I hung up, Molly passed me a mug filled over the top with whipped cream and chocolate drizzle.

"Chocolate makes everything better," Molly said. We sat on the stools in the kitchen and Molly listened intently as I told her about the last few days' events, everything from my meeting with Maren Bell at the school to the revelation about Dad to my gift from the killer.

"Why didn't you tell me all of this before?"

"It all seemed so unbelievable and I didn't want to pull you further into it. It seems like I'm constantly in trouble lately. You don't need that too,"

"It's more fun to be in trouble with a friend," she said. "You still haven't told me when you and Detective Graham developed a relationship. Please tell me it was after Rowan Wesley's accusations."

"Yes," I said. "I ran into him at the gym after everything went down and he told me Kelsey and he broke up and he was suspended for sixty days.

I apologized for causing so much trouble in his life and then that's when he told me he had feelings for me, too."

Molly, who'd been leaning on the counter top, straightened. "Wow. You know, Elijah and I both could see it, but I never dreamt he would actually say something…or act on it."

"Well, it's not what you think. He asked Mom if we could go out after I turned eighteen, and not before, and she agreed. He's determined to respect her wishes. But, all of that is only teenage drama compared to the killer sending me his souvenir."

"And naming it after you," Molly said and shuddered.

"Alec wants us to steer clear of Elijah and Declan for a while."

"Elijah is my boyfriend and there is no way he is responsible for this," she said, as she frowned at me over the top of her mug.

"It's only for a little while until Detective Tudor has a chance to investigate both of them. Although I told him, it couldn't be Declan either. I saw the look of awe on his face when he saw that piece. He wanted to know what the backing consisted of and he took it home with him for a few days."

"What did Detective, I mean Alec, say about that?"

"I asked if I should call Declan to warn him, but Alec said he would take care of him."

"Hmmm," Molly said, as she stirred her hot cocoa. "He doesn't like Declan, does he?"

"No, I really don't think he does. But I went out with Declan today and he seems like a great guy, handsome and funny. I can't picture him consorting with demons and carving out people's tattoos."

"Me either. Or Elijah, for that matter. Who does that leave?"

"No one I know," I replied with a shrug, before I lowered my voice in case Mrs. Hiroto walked into the kitchen. "You know what's even scarier? Alec told me the framed tattoos are similar to skin books. Do you know what those are?"

"Ew. Of course, I know what skin books are. Mom watches those documentaries all the time. They're right up her alley. I'm surprised your mom hasn't written a book about them yet."

"Well, I didn't know what they were. The Artist is doing that with his victims too, except he's creating art pieces."

Molly grabbed her phone from the kitchen counter. "Because he's obviously sick. There was a famous duo, two guys, about a hundred years ago in Scotland who murdered people and then sold their bodies to the local medical school as cadavers. Eventually, they were caught and one of them was hanged. Here it is," Molly said, as she held her phone up for me to see a YouTube video. "When the police captured them, one of them snitched, but this man, William Burke, was publicly hanged and then dissected and turned into a skin book and other items. They still exist today."

I watched in horror and admittedly fascination as the host of the video told the story of William Burke and William Hare and the murders in Edinburgh. I had to give it to the British hostess. She tried to make the gruesome segment entertaining.

"Not sure I'll be able to sleep after that," I remarked, as I took another sip of my now cold cocoa.

"I haven't been able to sleep since we found that woman. I swear every night I have dreams about finding her body," Molly whispered, as her eyes glazed over. "Sometimes, it's not her body I find. It's my own."

I'd never thought about it until now. I hadn't dreamt about the creatures or the victims or the framed pieces of flesh. As terrible as all of this was, it didn't affect me like I would've thought. Apparently, skin books were another matter entirely.

As if suddenly pulled back into the kitchen from a dream world, Molly poured her cocoa out and rinsed her cup. "Well, let's go upstairs and see if we can find you something amazing to wear to school tomorrow."

CHAPTER ELEVEN

The next morning at school was uneventful until third period when the crackle and pop of the intercom announced that Ainsley Reynolds was needed in the office. My chemistry teacher motioned for me to go and I gathered up my things and hurried to the office.

What now?

The secretary and Mr. Clendenin stood in the office, apparently waiting for me with strained expressions. Without a word, Mr. Clendenin nodded his head towards his office door and I followed him in. Detective Tudor and a female officer I didn't recognize sat in the seats across from the Vice-Principal's desk.

"Ainsley, this is Detective Wallace," Detective Tudor introduced me to the young woman.

"Hi," I said as I half-smiled at the new detective. "What's this about?" I asked Mr. Clendenin.

Mr. Clendenin motioned for me to have a seat. "Ainsley, I called your mother to join us, but the detectives with the Locklyn Police Department need to ask you a few questions. Questions that can't wait."

"What is it?" I addressed Detective Tudor.

The man furrowed his brow at a piece of paper in his hand before he met my gaze. "This has not been made public yet. None of your classmates know, but they will shortly. We've found another body."

"Oh God," I whispered.

"It was Derek Killian's body," the detective continued.

"Derek? I just saw him here at school Tuesday." I covered my mouth. "Poor Bronwyn," I said more to myself than to the adults in the room. She and Derek were a couple for a very long time. Well that was before Monday and although she was angry with him, I knew she missed him.

"Was it the same killer as the other victims?" I asked.

Detective Tudor and Detective Wallace exchanged glances. Mr. Clendenin pressed his lips together into a grim line.

"When your mother arrives, we'll have to go to the station for further questioning," Detective Tudor answered.

I blinked.

"Why?"

"We have some questions for you and we need clarification about your whereabouts. As well as those of Alec Graham's."

"My whereabouts? You think I had something to do with Derek's death? I haven't seen him since Tuesday and that was briefly passing in the hall. As for Alec, he is *your* partner. You know him. Call him." I was angry. Did the police really think I had something to do with this?

"I would, but I need you to tell me where Alec Graham is," Detective Tudor said, as he steadily held my gaze.

"I don't know where he is this morning. I haven't talked with him all day. Didn't he call you last night?"

"No, he didn't."

I was confused. "Alec didn't call you last night to inform you of the gift I'd received?"

Detective Tudor shook his head as Mom came through the office door.

"Stella," Mr. Clendenin greeted her as he stood up and came around the desk.

"Nick, what's going on here?" Mom demanded, as she not only eyeballed me, but the two detectives, who both stood as well.

"Mrs. Reynolds, I'm sorry to have to ask Mr. Clendenin to send for you, but we need to question Ainsley down at the station. It's about the recent victim found earlier this morning," Detective Tudor said, as he motioned for Mom to sit in the only empty chair in the room.

Mom ignored his request. "What does that have to do with Ainsley?" she asked, and then turned on me. "You told me you were spending the night at Molly's."

"I did, but they found a new body. And it's Derek Killian, Bronwyn's ex-boyfriend."

Mom gasped. "Why would you need to question her at the station?" Mom asked pointedly to Detective Tudor.

"We're trying to get clarification. Unfortunately, Ainsley and Alec Graham both had motive in Derek Killian's death."

"That's ridiculous," Mom and I said in unison.

Detective Tudor exhaled loudly. "Instead of going to the station, do I have your permission to question Ainsley here and now?" he asked, clearly aggravated with the Reynolds women.

"As long as I am in the room," Mom agreed, as she finally sat in the empty chair near the Vice-Principal. She and Mr. Clendenin exchanged glances. It appeared to be a look of support for the widow, with the unruly-of-late daughter, from the man who ruled Locklyn High with a strict code.

Detective Tudor gestured to Detective Wallace to hand him the manila folder the woman held. Once he had it, he carefully slid out what appeared to be photographs in plastic.

"What is the nature of your relationship with Alec Graham?" he asked me.

"He was the detective investigating this case, and then we became friends," I answered.

"Are you more than friends?" he asked, and I could hear the disdain in his voice.

"Not in the sense that you are implying. We are currently friends, but we have discussed exploring that relationship in the future. After I turn eighteen." I glared at the man as Mom shifted slightly in her chair.

"Did you or did you not threaten Derek Killian Monday after he exposed your relationship with Detective Graham?"

"What do you mean?"

"Other students heard you say to Derek Killian and Rowan Wesley that they both would "get the Hell that they deserve," he stated, as he referred to his notebook balancing on his lap.

"I may have yelled something like that, but I wasn't threatening them bodily harm," I replied.

"But you were angry?"

"Of course, I was angry. They were lying and making unfounded accusations," I said, and turned to Mom. "We've been through this."

"Detective Tudor," Mom interjected. "It's already been established that Alec and Ainsley handled the situation badly and as far as I know, Detective Graham accepted a suspension. Ainsley doesn't hold any ill feelings towards Rowan or Derek."

"Hmmm," the detective said, as he handed me the photos.

Mom leaned over as I stared in shock at the pictures. Rowan didn't take these photographs. One photo was of Alec and me on his front porch Saturday morning with his back to the street. It was snapped while he stretched. That meant the photograph was taken from directly across the street. I wracked my memory. A neighbor had parked their car across the street and went inside their house. It'd been a man with a hat on. I hadn't seen his face and I'd assumed he lived there. Was this taken from inside that house? Or, from the car?

The second photograph showed me in Alec's SUV yesterday evening in the gym parking lot. The photographer had zoomed in at the moment Alec and I had kissed.

Mom let out an exasperated sigh.

I flipped back to the first photo as I stared at Alec's back. "Who took these?" I asked.

Detective Wallace answered. "We don't know. They were left at the crime scene early this morning."

"Where is Detective Graham, Ainsley?" Detective Tudor asked.

"I don't know, but he wouldn't bother with Derek. Why would he?"

"Derek Killian and Rowan Wesley cost him a great deal. They earned him a suspension on an otherwise spotless record. He and his girlfriend parted ways because of his relationship with you that he wanted to keep secret. We've already spoken with her this morning. Maybe he had enough of nosy kids upsetting his life," he said.

"You don't believe that," I seethed, a little more hateful than I meant to. "You know him better than that."

"How was Derek's body found?" Mom asked. "Was it like the others?"

Detective Tudor shifted in his chair this time. "Yes. The tattoo Derek Killian had on his arm was in a frame with his body posed to admire the artwork. Like the others."

"Well, there you go," Mom commented. "Do you really believe that Alec has the means to copycat such a horrible murder?"

"We can't comment on that, Ma'am," Detective Wallace interjected.

"I bet you can't," Mom retorted, as she shook her head at Mr. Clendenin.

"Alec was supposed to call you last night to tell you about the artwork I'd received. You never got the call?" I asked.

"I didn't receive a call from *Detective Graham*. Why don't you tell me about this artwork?" he asked. Apparently, he didn't like me addressing Detective Graham as Alec.

"Over the weekend, I received a gift in the mail. It was a piece of artwork made in a handcrafted and detailed frame, so I assumed it was from an artist I'd met at Queens University. But the artist denied it was from him. I'd shown *Alec* a picture of the piece and last night he said the artwork matched the lower back tattoo of the female victim. The one that wasn't found with the body."

"How did he know what the female victim's tattoo looked like?" Detective Tudor asked.

"You sent him a picture of it," I replied slowly. Maybe Detective Tudor was daft. Or, this was some sort of test.

"I never sent Detective Graham a picture of the evidence," he growled.

"Yes, you did," I answered, my voice rising. "I saw your text. It was the picture of the woman when she was alive wearing a bikini. A picture her family sent to the police from her Facebook. That's why Alec was calling you last night."

"I can't discuss the case with Detective Graham while he's on suspension, Ainsley," Detective Tudor said, and his jaw hardened.

None of this made any sense. Was Detective Tudor lying to cover his own hide because he did ask Alec for his input in the case? I couldn't tell him I'd overheard his conversation at Alec's house that he would text him images of the framed art – not without confessing that I'd been in the guest bedroom. And admitting I was secretly in a bedroom at Alec's house would not go over well with anyone.

"So, you said Alec Graham was supposed to call Detective Tudor last night," Detective Wallace remarked. "How do you know that? Were you with him? Or did you talk to him?"

Crap. I bit my lip as I rolled my eyes over to Mom.

Her mouth dropped open and she shook her head at me.

"I had a date with the art student from Queens University yesterday afternoon, but I'd already spoken to Alec earlier and he was worried about me. We thought it was a good idea if I learned to protect myself. So, after my date, Alec and I went to the gun range and he taught me how to fire at a target. This photo must have been taken in front of the gym before we left for the range." I ran my hand over the picture of me kissing Alec.

Mom covered her mouth, but didn't say anything.

"What time was that?" the younger detective asked.

"From about four to eight, then I went to my friend Molly's house to spend the night after Alec received the text from you," I said, as I nodded at Detective Tudor.

"I never sent Detective Graham a text last night," Detective Tudor barked.

I pulled my phone out of my back pocket. "Oh really? Well, I saw it. The tattoo on the girl's back looked like this," I said, as I thrust my phone at the two detectives. It was set on the image of the artwork from the killer.

Detective Wallace took my phone and zoomed in as she studied the picture. "Where is this piece? Do you have it?"

"Not right now. My artist friend asked to borrow it for a few days."

"Can you provide me with his info? If this is what I think it is, we don't need your friend contaminating evidence," she commanded in a stern tone.

"Of course," I said. "But, Mom and I both handled it as well. We even hung it up in my room for a few days."

Detective Wallace nodded her head as I took my phone back and jotted Declan's contact info on a piece of paper.

As the detective made notes in her notebook, I flipped back to the photograph of Alec sitting on his front porch bannister. With his arms outstretched, every detail of his tattoo was perfect.

Picture perfect.

"Oh my God," I said.

"What is it?" Mom asked.

"None of us have heard from Alec today," I announced to the room. I stood up as I pointed to the photograph. "Whoever took this photo wasn't capturing me at Alec's house Saturday morning. I think they wanted to capture his tattoo in the picture."

The detectives exchanged glances.

"What if Alec is missing because the killer got to him last night? What if this was left as a message?" I asked, and then added quietly as tears streamed down my face, "What if Alec's the next victim?"

"We're considering that, but it's unlikely," Detective Wallace said as she stood.

Detective Tudor stood as well as he gathered the photographic evidence. "Ainsley, you need to consider another theory. A theory with a great deal of evidence behind it. It's very probable that Detective Graham is working with the murderer to feed him inside information on the case."

"He wouldn't do that," I choked up as I broke down in tears. Mom put her arm around me and pulled me into a hug.

The detectives moved towards the door. Detective Tudor nodded at Mr. Clendenin before he addressed me again. "You can't make that assumption. You only met him last week. Alec Graham is trained and ex-military. It would take some doing to catch him off guard and take him out. We don't believe our murderer would resort to that type of physical confrontation. None of the victims had any bruises, only their wounds from the removal of their tattoos. Plus, there was an incident right before Detective Graham moved here from Wilmington that proves he can be violent if provoked. Listen, it's important that if he contacts you, you call me. For now, until we have a different lead, do not go anywhere with Alec Graham."

~ ~ ~

After the detectives left, I struggled to regain my composure in front of Mr. Clendenin. I refused to believe what Detective Tudor suggested about Alec. If he was working with the killer, then why would he teach me how to shoot a gun?

"Nick, I think it would be best if I take Ainsley home before the announcement about Derek," Mom said, as she helped me gather my things.

"Of course," he replied, as he walked around to the front of his desk. Then I watched as the Vice-Principal of my school embraced my mother in a hug.

"I'm so sorry all of this is happening, Stella. If there is anything I can do, will you please call me? Not as the Vice-Principal, but as your friend."

Mom nodded and thanked him before we headed out of the office. Thankfully, classes were still in session. I couldn't bear the idea of coming face to face with Bronwyn after she learned of Derek's death.

Mom was quiet during most of the trip home which gave me a chance to mull over the detectives' accusations and the two photographs.

"Before you say it, I'm the one who kissed him last night in the parking lot," I said.

"Well, if he was trying to escape your clutches, it didn't show in the picture. I understand why you went to the gun range with Alec last night, although you didn't tell me. But, it is vitally important that you do what Detective Tudor told you. If Alec calls or stops by, we have to call the police," Mom warned, as she turned onto our street.

"He didn't do this," I answered.

"It sounds like he's the prime suspect in these murders, at least as an accomplice. Apparently, he's their only lead."

"They're so bent on making him a killer that they're not really looking for him as a possible victim," I said and willed myself not to cry. "It doesn't make any sense. Why would he want me to protect myself? Why teach me to shoot? To protect myself from him?"

Mom frowned as she pulled the car into the garage. She parked and shut off the engine before she turned to answer. "Hear me out. What if Alec was working with the murderer for some reason, but they had a falling out? Maybe because of you. The art piece sent to you may have been a warning or a message to Alec. Let's say, maybe he put two and two together last night and either took off or confronted the murderer."

I wiped away a tear. "This is why you're the writer. But, I really don't believe Alec would do such a thing. If you only knew him…"

"Like you do? Detective Tudor is right as much as I hate to admit it. We've only known these people for a little over a week. We can't assume anything," she said, as she got out of the car.

That part was true. So many new people had entered our lives in the last week and a half. I'd assumed everyone was honest and trustworthy. But what if the killer was someone I'd never met?

I walked upstairs and into the kitchen, thinking about what Maren had told me. Serial killers liked to play games, like cat and mouse. They like to get close, so you don't see them for who they are until it's too late.

"Mom?"

Mom turned on the news and sank into the couch as the reporter announced the body found this morning on the outskirts of town in a barn belonged to Locklyn High School Senior, Derek Killian. Locklyn High School would dismiss three hours early today and counselors would be on hand.

"Mom? Do you think Ms. Bell would see me today for a counseling session?"

Mom raised her eyes to meet mine. "That might be a good idea. I'll text her, although she might be overwhelmed with sessions at the school."

I nodded and then went to my room. Students would probably want to talk to her about Derek. I decided to send her a text.

I think the Muladach, the demons, have influenced the killer to take Alec. He's missing. Can you pick me up for a "counseling session" so we can discuss what I can do to help find him? Before it's too late?

According to Raymond Moore, the Muladach could influence the killer, but they could also trick the victim into laying down their life without a fight. That would explain why the victims didn't have any bruises anywhere else on their bodies. They'd willingly gone to their deaths. They probably posed themselves however the killer liked for the presentation of the "art."

I pulled Alec's name up on my phone and pressed the call button. It went straight to voicemail. I listened to his voice and at once missed him.

"Alec, where are you? The police came to the school today. They think you had something to do with Derek Killian's death. I need you to please call me back. I'm scared for you."

I waited ten minutes with the hope that Alec would call me. Even a text would suffice.

Nothing.

I decided to take a chance and call Declan. The phone rang five times before it went to voicemail. "Hi Declan. It's Ainsley. Can you give me a call back when you can? It's about the artwork. Thanks."

I pressed end and stared out my bedroom window. What could I do? The police were not treating Alec as a missing person, but rather a suspect. Had the demons influenced him to go somewhere?

As I turned away from the window, I caught a glimpse of the picture of Dad and me. I plucked it off the desk and took it over to my bed as I sat and crossed my legs. My finger traced over the pendant around Dad's neck.

What would Dad have done in this situation? Was it possible for the Muladach to influence Alec while he wore the necklace? Maren believed that the medallion protected Dad from the demonic forces during investigations. Maybe it would do the same for Alec.

My phone beeped softly and I jumped to grab it off the blanket. It was a text, but not from Alec or Declan. It was from Maren.

Yes. I can swing by and pick you up in a few hours, probably around six or so. Lots of students need me right now. Try to clear your mind. Can you feel the demon's energy? If so, you may be able to lead the police to the next crime scene.

I wanted to respond with **The next crime scene? You mean Alec's body.**

But a sarcastic answer wouldn't help anyone right now, especially Alec or the grieving students at Locklyn High. I simply text back **OK**. I didn't feel any vibration or energy, not like I had at the junior high school or the art exhibit.

I called Bronwyn next, but hung up before she answered. I honestly didn't know what to say to her. Instead I called Molly. She picked up on the first ring.

"Hey, girl. I'm still in shock over Derek, and Bronwyn's a mess. Her mom had to come pick her up from school. Maxie told me you left during third period," Molly said.

"I didn't have time to tell you. The police were in Mr. Clendenin's office to question me about Derek and Alec."

"Why you?"

"They erroneously believe that Alec and I had a motive. I think they're convinced now that I couldn't possibly have anything to do with this, but they think I know where Alec's gone. Apparently, he didn't call Detective Tudor last night and no one can find him today."

"Are you serious? Do you think he killed Derek?" Molly asked, and I pictured her freaked out, standing on her bed in her room.

"No, I'd swear my life on it. Someone left photos with Derek's body of Alec and me. One of the pictures was of Alec's tattoo. The one on his back. Molly, I think the killer somehow got to Alec, but the police don't believe it."

"They don't think the murderer would go after Alec over his tat like the others? Why not?"

"They said Alec is highly trained and it would be almost impossible for someone to get the jump on him. But maybe the killer does have a highly-trained accomplice and that person was able to get to him," I suggested, as I rubbed my temples. My head throbbed from the worry and stress.

"Maybe. But, Ainsley, what if the cops are right? What if Alec was involved with the murders on some level? You could be in serious danger."

I sat stunned on the edge of the bed. My best friend doubted Alec's innocence.

"I'm not joking, Ainsley. You need to allow the possibility to take root that Alec might be the murderer, or at least, an accomplice. Think about it; what do you really know about him?"

I laid back on the bed and closed my eyes.

"Detective Tudor spoke of something that happened in Wilmington that proved Alec could be violent if provoked. I know he was trained in the military and served overseas during his time in the Marines. He jumped through the Police Academy and promoted from officer to detective faster than anyone else. He's investigated some of the highest profile cases in the area and his service record is what landed him the position as the youngest homicide detective in Locklyn," I answered.

"When did he start paying attention to you?" Molly asked. "More than just as a witness? Was it after you'd gone to his home and told him about the creatures?"

"I guess it was," I replied, as I remembered his smile and wink at the school when he picked me up to view the surveillance videos. "Last night ,he told me I might be the target because I could see the demons and that could lead the police to the killer. He said I was a liability. Molly, he called someone last night. I heard the ringing through the speakerphone. If he didn't call Detective Tudor, then who was it?"

I didn't say it out loud to Molly, but was it possible that Alec called the killer? Was the artwork a message to Alec that my life was under threat if he didn't cooperate?

"Ainsley? Are you still there?" Molly asked in my ear.

"Yes. I'm trying to put the pieces together. Trying to see if Alec fits into the puzzle."

"And does he?"

I sat up as tears spilled down my face. "Yes, it all fits. But, I don't feel it in my gut. I don't feel like he's the one doing all of this."

"Maybe that's because you're too close," Molly said.

"Wouldn't you be? What if everyone thought Elijah was responsible?" I asked, as I wiped the mess of tears and mascara onto the back of my hand.

"If you remember, Alec sort of accused him last night. Told us to stay away from Elijah and Declan."

"Only because he didn't trust them since we'd just met last week," I said.

"Yet, Elijah isn't the one the police suspect," she retorted.

I was quiet for a moment. She was right. Alec had said the police were looking into Declan, but he didn't say anything about Elijah. "Have you talked to Elijah today?"

"No. I tried calling to tell him about Derek, but he didn't answer. I left him a voicemail and sent him a text. My guess is he's caught up with classes and assignments. You know, midterms."

"I left a voicemail for Declan today too. I wanted to tell him to stop examining the artwork before the police show up at his door to confiscate it. It's evidence. He hasn't called me back either."

"Do you think they're okay?" Molly asked. "What if the murderer realized Declan had the artwork, and got worried that the police might be able to trace it back? It's odd that neither one of them has called, or at least, sent a text."

"I don't know. What should we do? I don't think the police will do anything about it."

"I say we go to Charlotte. We check up on the boys ourselves. Why wait for the police? It's probably nothing. Elijah and Declan are probably studying, but I'd feel better to see that for myself."

"Okay, but I have to be back by six. I'm supposed to meet with Ms. Bell, but I'll text her that we're headed to Queens. What time are you picking me up?"

"Give me about twenty minutes," Molly answered.

As soon as I hung up from her, I texted Maren. Within minutes, I was on the phone with her.

"I don't know if that is such a good idea, Ainsley. To go to Charlotte now? Especially, since the police found your friend's body this morning."

"We're only going to Queens University to check on Elijah and Declan. Nowhere else. We're worried about them, and you know, the police are not going to take me seriously," I said, as I put my phone on speakerphone in order to grab my backpack and empty it out onto the bed.

"Sounds like you're pretty set on going no matter what I say," Maren responded. Thank Heavens we weren't on a video call, so she couldn't see me roll my eyes. "Your father was the same way."

When I didn't answer her, she added, "Why don't you at least let me drive you two girls? It'll give me the chance to talk with you. We need to see if you can channel your energy to find this cluster of demons. And maybe find your detective friend."

I stuffed my purse and a lightweight jacket into my backpack. "Yes, that's what I want to do. But Molly is ready to leave now. She'll be here any minute."

"Meet me at my home. I'll text your mother back and let her know I'm going to hold a counseling session for both of you girls."

I glanced at Dad's picture on my bed. He wouldn't be happy that I continued to lie to Mom. But, then again, the man who was my hero my entire life had gone on the occasional "business trip" to fight the creatures as a demonologist. According to Maren, Gerald "Gerry" Reynolds was the best.

And whether I liked it or not, I seemed destined to follow in his footsteps.

I only prayed it wasn't too late to save Alec.

CHAPTER TWELVE

"**N**o offense, Ms. Bell, but I think we should've taken my car. It's not as…compact," Molly said, as she shifted her legs in the back of Maren's blue Fiat.

"You can call me Maren outside of school, Molly. And I like my car. It's perfect for me and it's great on gas for a short trip like this," Maren answered, as she kept her eyes on the road. We'd only had to wait for her to change clothes, and grab Dad's box, before we left, so we were making good time.

"Do you think we'll need to use the things in the box?" I asked.

"Hopefully, not. But the way demon clusters work is they drive the host insane and make promises until they reach a feverish pitch. If they are influencing this murderer, then he'll become bolder until the end. The box may help. I wish you had your father's medallion."

"Dad's medallion may be the only thing protecting Alec right now. We don't know."

"Unless it's him," Molly quipped.

I spun around in my seat. "It's not him. I don't care how things line up. I know it deep down that it's not him," I said through clenched teeth.

"Then I guess, pray he's still alive because the other victims were killed not long after they were taken, according to my mother – including Derek," Molly said, as she glared back at me.

"Arguing over the detective's guilt or innocence isn't helpful right now," Maren scolded. "It's the demon cluster controlling the murderer. We find the cluster and use Gerry's objects from the box to send them back to Hell. Then if we know who the murderer is, we'll contact the police."

I bit my tongue from commenting on Maren's use of the word *Gerry*. "How do we use these things for that? I don't want to confront those creatures again. They came after me the other day and I couldn't see them. If I *can* see them up close, like that statue, I'm probably going to be too terrified to move."

"Open the box," Maren instructed, as she sped up to pass a Mustang in the middle lane.

Molly pulled on my seat to scoot forward as I slowly removed the lid to Dad's box. The papers were stacked on the right side with the scroll on top. The two heavy crosses and the purple cloth were on the left side.

"Pull out the scroll. You need to go over it," Maren said.

"Now? We're only going to the college to check on the guys," I said, as I pulled the scroll out and wedged the box next to my feet.

Maren sighed loudly. "Must you question everything I ask you to do? The truth is we don't know what we're going to find in Charlotte or when we get back to Locklyn. It worries me more that you haven't felt the demons nearby for a few days - yet Derek is dead, and your Alec is missing. If Gerry was here, he would tell you that it's a bad sign when the demons go quiet."

"Why is that a bad sign?" Molly asked, since I'd lost all sense of speech from Maren's outburst.

"It means the demon cluster may be done with their host. He may have finished whatever mission the demons had him on."

"One final victim," I whispered.

"If we're lucky," Maren said. "Sometimes it's a group of people lost in a final demonstration of evil."

I unrolled the scroll. "What can I do?'

"You're going to learn to read Latin. Right now. Then if you're confronted by a demon, you can expel it back to Hell."

"I can't memorize Latin in a day."

Molly leaned forward in the seat. "Maybe you don't have to memorize it. Do you still have a Sharpie in your bag? We'll write it on your arm."

"I emptied my bag at home. Would that work?" I asked Maren.

"As long as you can say the words at the right time, it doesn't matter if you're saying them from memory, reading from the scroll, or reciting off your arm for that matter. But we need to go over them now. Molly, pop open that cannister in the floor of the backseat. It's some of my classroom supplies. I always have to buy more. There's never enough in the budget," Maren grumbled, as she floored the little Fiat down the fast lane.

~ ~ ~

I was grateful I'd worn a long sleeve shirt today from Molly's closet to hide my left forearm. I'd covered the inside of it with the Latin words from the scroll as Maren had instructed. I was slow in reading the passage, but by the time we reached Queens University, I was doing better.

And so was Molly. She'd helped me memorize some of the words as I read them dozens of times.

As we pulled onto the parking lot near Elijah's dorm, I placed the scroll back into the box. "Did Dad memorize this passage to expel demons?" I asked Maren.

"Your father was fluent in Latin, so he didn't have any problem memorizing specific passages or prayers."

I wasn't sure why, but my heart sank a little. "My father never uttered a single word in Latin in my presence. As a matter of fact, he made jokes about me taking French in middle school. He thought I needed to learn a language I'm more likely to use in our area. Like Spanish.

Maren parked the car and switched off the engine before she turned to look at me. Her mouth turned downward and for a moment, I thought she was going to cry.

"Gerry spoke Latin as well as Spanish and Dari. He told me he'd learned Dari while stationed in Afghanistan and he was glad he did because he ran up against a demon cluster using a twelve-year old boy to slay soldiers while they slept. No one suspected the boy. Your father didn't go into much detail about what happened, but when he told me it was the only time I ever saw him cry."

I blinked. My father had *cried* in front of Maren? Had I ever seen my father cry? I wasn't sure. Maybe when Ben was born, and he was super proud to be the father of a son, but that was tears of joy. Not because he may or may not have had to kill a boy overseas.

"Come on, Ains," Molly said, as she reached over the seat and swept my hair away from my face. "Let's go find Elijah and Declan."

At her words, I quickly recovered from the shock and growing anger and disappointment with my dad, who'd kept an entire life secret from his family. At least, he hadn't cheated on Mom with Maren or fathered multiple children around the globe. He located and expelled demons. Things could've been much worse in my opinion.

We crossed the street and headed to the brick building that housed Elijah's dorm. Hopefully, everything was fine, and he could point us in the direction of Declan.

"I've text him three times that we're coming, but he still hasn't answered me," Molly said, as she walked at an almost sprint. I had trouble keeping up with her.

"Do you know where we're going? What's his dorm room number?" I asked her.

"Room 204. I'm praying he forgot to turn his phone off silent," she answered, as she pulled the door open to the building. Maren and I followed her as she rushed to the elevator.

Molly patted her leg as the elevator made its short ride to the second floor. I didn't know what to say to her to calm her nerves. I felt the same way about Alec, but at least we had a head start on where to find Elijah. I didn't know where to begin to look for Alec.

The doors opened onto a small narrow hallway. Maren and I followed Molly down past oak doors until she found Room 204. She knocked loudly three times.

Silence.

This time she banged the wooden door so hard, the wood threatened to crack. "Elijah?"

We heard the elevator's ding and the doors opened as if to answer Molly. There stood Elijah with a boy I didn't recognize. They stepped off the elevator.

"Molly? What are you doing here?" Elijah asked, clearly shocked to see her.

She ran to him and threw her arms around his neck. His friend laughed and shook his head as he made his way past us. "You're safe! Why didn't you answer my calls and texts?" she asked, as she held onto him for dear life.

Elijah kissed her lightly on the lips. "Sorry, I lost my phone yesterday. I had it in Art class, but when I gathered my things to leave, it was gone. I've looked everywhere. I'm heading to the Apple store tomorrow to buy another one, I guess." He turned to me. "Are you telling me you guys made a trip all the way here because I didn't answer my phone?"

"It's more than that," I said. "Have you seen Declan?"

"Not since class yesterday. Why?"

"He hasn't returned my call either."

"We believe the boy might be in danger," Maren added.

"Oh, yes," Molly said, as she pulled herself off Elijah. "This is Maren Bell, our Psych teacher. She's also a counselor. One of our friends was found dead this morning. It's believed it was the same killer terrorizing Locklyn."

"The one posing the victims? I saw it on the news. I'm so sorry," Elijah said, as he pulled Molly closer.

"Maybe we could talk about all of this after we find your friend Declan," Maren suggested.

"Of course," Elijah answered. "Let me just toss my bag into my room. Come on."

We followed him back to his room and waited for him to unlock the door. It was exactly what I pictured a dorm room to look like. There was a twin-size bed, a dresser, a bookcase, and a desk. Of course, Elijah had made it his own with artwork on the walls, small sculptures on the bookcase, and a colorful comforter on the bed. There was also an easel by the window and a large plastic bin with drawers that held his art supplies.

He threw his bag onto the bed, and then checked to make sure he had his wallet in his back pocket. "I'm still confused," he said. "Why would you think I was in danger? Or Declan?"

"I received a gift in the mail on Sunday, a framed piece of artwork with a woman sitting beside a pond," I answered. "I thought it was from Declan because of the frame, but he denied it and thought maybe it was from you."

Elijah frowned.

"That's what I thought. Anyway, Declan asked if he could borrow the piece for a few days because he was curious about the backing material. I showed a picture of the artwork to the police this morning and it matches the lower back tattoo from the female victim. The one we found at the school. The killer sent it to me for some reason."

"Not only that," Molly interjected. "But, our friend Derek was murdered, and Detective Graham is missing. We're afraid that if the murderer knows that Ainsley gave the piece to Declan, he may go after him to get it back. The police may be able to trace it."

Elijah's mouth dropped open. "This is insane. Can they do that?"

"Insane or not, it's reality," Maren said. "We need to find Declan, so we can confirm he is all right, and if we can, get the artwork back so we can give it to the police. The murderer sent it to Ainsley for a reason. Perhaps, as a warning or a threat, but she may be the only one that can stop all of this."

"How? Why you?" he asked.

"The murderer isn't working alone. He's being influenced by the very creatures your brother saw. They're real, Elijah. They're demons. And there's more than one," I answered.

Maren placed her hand on the knob of the bedroom door. "Right. Ainsley has inherited a gift from her father that enables her to sense their presence, sometimes she can see them. She now has the tools to stop them, but we're wasting time talking here. We need to find the boy, so we can head back to Locklyn and try to locate Alec."

"I can't believe they're real," Elijah said, as he grabbed his pocket knife off the dresser and slid it into his pocket. He looked at me. "Just in case."

"Good," I said. "Except, I highly doubt a pocket knife will stop a demon."

"Maybe not. But it can kill a person."

~ ~ ~

When we stepped outside, I shivered as the frigid air whipped through my shirt. In my hurry to find Elijah, I'd forgotten to grab my jacket out of my backpack. We'd left my bag and Dad's box in the car.

"Where do we start?" I asked.

"Declan is usually in one of three places. His apartment, the art studio, or the food court. Let's split up. Molly and I will trek over to the Art Studio. It's only a couple of buildings down. You two can head over to Declan's place. It's Apartment Six in the white building across the street from Pearl Hall." Elijah pointed down the street which narrowed our search as there were only two brick buildings on the left. Apartment buildings and parking lots lined up the right-hand side of the street.

Maren and I both nodded as Elijah and Molly headed in the opposite direction. We quickened our pace as we got closer to Pearl Hall.

"There. That must be the building," Maren said, and pointed to a white two-story apartment complex. Three doors which I assumed led to three apartments and a bannister made up the ground floor. The floor above was identical.

We crossed the street and I glanced around, but it seemed that most of the residential students were already inside their dorm rooms or apartments. This section of the campus was quiet. A wooden stairwell jutted out from the side of the building and we climbed it to the narrow balcony. Sure enough, Apartment Six was the last door. I opened the screen door and knocked.

After about thirty seconds, I knocked again.

"Maybe Molly and Elijah are having more luck," Maren said.

I turned the knob and realized the door was unlocked, but before I could push the door more than an inch, it emanated an electrical shock that moved through my hand and up into my arm. It traveled into my shoulder, pushing me with such a strong force, that I yelped as it escaped out my collarbone.

"What's wrong?" Maren asked, as she caught me from falling backwards off the balcony.

I touched my shoulder and then examined my hand. No blood. No gaping hole in my shoulder.

"There was an electrical shock. It was a vibration so strong that it felt like it blew a hole right through me," I whispered.

"They're here," Maren said, as she scanned the area. "The demon cluster is here. Your father felt the same thing when he got too close to a powerful group."

"Where are you going?" I asked Maren, as she turned away and hurried to the stairs.

"We need your father's box."

"We need to get inside," I urged. "If they're this powerful now, then every second counts in finding Declan and Alec."

"Just wait here for me. I'll be right back. Don't go inside yet," Maren said over her shoulder, as she descended the stairs at a run.

What would Dad have done? Would he have waited for back-up if someone's life was in danger? Or, would he have snuck in quietly, assessed the situation, and acted accordingly? But I wasn't a Marine. I didn't have the nerve.

Yes, I do. I'm my Father's daughter. I'm stronger than I think. I will hold my ground against this evil. Because that's what he would do. That's what he would expect me to do.

I pushed the door open and ignored the painful shock it sent through my arm again. The open living room and kitchen areas were a mess. I stepped in and surveyed the knocked over chair and stools, the shattered glass coffee table, the broken ceramics. The artwork on the walls were either crooked or on the floor.

There'd been a struggle between Declan and someone else...or something else. Apparently, he'd fought hard. I carefully stepped over the broken items and walked to the hall. I peeked into the only bathroom and then the bedroom. Both were empty and neat. The fight must've stayed in the living room and kitchen. I backtracked my steps and headed for the door until I saw the glint of silver on the floor near the wall.

No, it couldn't be.

I stepped over the broken glass and reached for the silver chain on the carpet. As I pulled the broken chain and pendant up to my face, I gasped. It was Dad's medallion.

I observed the room again, this time with fresh eyes. Alec had been here. Had he fought Declan? Why? The What-If questions ran through my mind faster than I could process as a new sensation filled my chest. A horrible and terrifying dread. Had Alec come here last night after he dropped me off at Molly's?

I examined the carpet a little closer. Small dried reddish-black drops peppered the spot where I'd found the necklace. It was also on the white wall. I certainly wasn't a forensics investigator like Mrs. Hiroto, but I was pretty sure this was someone's blood. And it was dry. Probably from last night or early this morning.

I stood up. This didn't bode well for either man. But where was the framed artwork? The one the killer had sent me?

"Ainsley!" Maren's high-pitched whisper pulled me from my thoughts. She stood at the doorway with Dad's box in her arms, her eyes wide as she glanced around the room.

I shook my head as I walked towards her. "I couldn't wait. I had to be sure Declan wasn't in here hurt. But there's nothing here. Except this," I said, as I held up Dad's medallion.

Maren lowered her gaze before she answered. "Oh, honey, I'm so sorry. I'd hoped the police were wrong and that Alec was innocent."

"Hey." Molly poked her head around the door frame as Elijah took the box from Maren. "Did you find anything?" She sounded breathless. She and Elijah must have run to the apartment complex.

"This. It was Dad's."

Molly winced. "And you gave it to Alec."

I turned back to the living room and surveyed the mess. "Okay. Apparently, Declan fought someone. I guess it could've been Alec since the pendant is here. But *why* was Alec here?" I turned back to my friends. "Was it to get the frame from Declan? Was it to confront him?"

Molly stepped closer and pulled me into a hug. "Maybe Alec was here to get the frame back from Declan. Maybe he's helping The Artist for some insane reason."

I leaned away as I studied her face. Was Molly right?

Maren stepped into the room. "Or maybe Declan is The Artist, and the two of them fought over their involvement with you. Didn't you say you went out with Declan? Maybe they were one-upping each other until they realized that eventually the demons would lead you to *both* of them."

It certainly looked that way. I wanted to protest, but I lacked the proof. Everything pointed to Alec, and now maybe Declan too.

"I think we should call the police about this," Molly said, as she waved her hand at the room. "It's clear something has happened to Declan. If he's not The Artist, then he's in trouble."

Before I could answer her, I felt the sudden wave of energy move through the room. I watched as Molly's body rippled as if underwater. I grabbed for the door to steady myself as the air grew thicker, suffocating me. The ripple of energy pulled back and hovered over Elijah, who stood on the balcony still holding the box, and then whipped over to the buildings on the other side of the nearest parking lot.

"What is that building?" I asked Elijah ,when the vibration settled.

"It's the old Science building, but it's been closed for a year. The new one is a few blocks over."

I turned to Maren. "We need to go there. The energy is emanating from that building," I said, surprising myself with my sudden air of confidence.

"Are you sure?" Elijah asked.

"Yes. It came through like a wave or a pulse. Then it rebounded. I think your brother's Muladach is there." I tied the chain from Dad's pendant around my neck and knotted it. The clasp was broken, but I didn't care. Maybe it would protect me.

Elijah studied me before he nodded. "It's a large building. I think we should split up again. Molly and I will take the first floor and basement. You two should cover the second floor."

The four of us walked silently over to the rather enormous brick building. "How do we get in?" Molly asked.

Elijah set the box on one of the concrete steps as he pulled a cell phone out of his pocket.

"I thought you'd lost your phone?" I asked, as he tapped the screen for a few seconds and then peered up at the windows.

"I did. This one is a loaner from a friend. I think there's a door on the other side that will let us onto the first floor."

We walked around to the back of the building. I didn't like this side of the Science building at all. There were no apartment complexes or parking lots here. It was isolated. Sure enough, the side door was unlocked – just like at the schools.

We stood on the first floor and I listened intently. It was quiet.

Elijah pointed over to a set of double doors in the corner. "Those stairs lead up to the second floor."

"Okay, but we meet back here in thirty minutes," I said.

Elijah, Molly, and Maren nodded in agreement. Maren took Dad's box back from Elijah.

"Be careful," Molly said to me.

"You too," I answered, as Maren and I started towards the stairwell doors. We climbed the metal steps as quietly as we could to another set of double doors that opened to the second floor. The hallway was long and at first, I thought there was no way we could check all these rooms in a half hour, but door after door was locked. That is until we came to a large office with glass doors. These doors opened easily and led to a small hallway with doors on either side.

"Visitor and Scheduling Center," I read aloud the sign on the wall.

"You try the doors on the right. I'll do these." Maren pointed the box toward the doors on the left.

The first door led to a small office with another small corridor. I checked the rooms, but they were all empty. I walked back out into the main hallway and started for the next door when I heard a thud. It'd sounded like Maren had dropped Dad's box. I went back to the open door and stood in the doorway. The layout of this office was identical to the one across the hall. Maren must've walked into one of the smaller rooms.

"Maren?" I whispered, hopefully loud enough for her to hear, but not the demons. "Are you okay?"

She didn't answer.

I started down the corridor and chided myself for not bringing some type of weapon. A gun or knife wouldn't have made much of a difference to the Muladach, but I would've felt better.

I turned the knob to the first door and slowly opened it. "Maren?"

"Hello, Ainsley," a deep voice answered me. I jumped and then pushed the door further open. Maren was shoved against the wall with her arm pinned behind her back and a gun to her head. Detective David Tudor nodded his head toward me. His face was swollen and bruised. He wore a nasty cut across his forehead.

"Get in here and shut the door," he growled.

I swung the door shut behind me as I carefully maneuvered around Dad's open box on the floor, its contents spilled out.

"You're the accomplice," I said, as I blinked back tears. He still had the muzzle pressed against the side of Maren's head. She made eye contact with me and then glanced at the floor and back up to me again. What did she want me to do? I didn't have a gun.

"You weren't supposed to be here," he said. "But you couldn't leave well enough alone. You got Alec involved and he's like a dog with a bone."

"Where is he?" I whispered, afraid to know the answer.

"Probably dead by now. Or, close to it." The detective turned back to Maren and squeezed her arm. She yelped in pain.

"Why are you doing this?" I asked, as I took a step forward, hoping to get his attention away from Maren.

It worked because he swung the gun in my direction. "Do you have any idea what solving The Artist Case will do for my career? When I stop him, it'll open doors for me. Opportunities. Private work, FBI, you name it. He's almost finished with his Final Masterpiece and then I'll step in and save the day."

"Who told you that would happen?"

"The Artist, himself. He told me my future. He's almost finished and then he's ready to depart this world. Unfortunately, sacrifices must be made," he answered, as he raised the gun level to my face.

"No!" Maren screamed, as she pushed her legs against the wall and knocked Detective Tudor off balance. I dropped to the floor as I heard two gunshots. My hand wrapped around Dad's heavy gold cross and I hurled it upwards like a kettlebell. It caught the tall man in the face as he'd grabbed for my shirt. He fell backwards onto the tiled floor.

Maren was on the floor with her hand over her hip as she covered a growing red spot. I rushed to her side.

"You're shot," I said in a panic. I grabbed my cell phone and dialed 9-1-1 as I covered her hands with mine and pressed down. I'd seen it done in the movies a million times, but I wasn't sure if it would really stop the bleeding.

I told the 9-1-1 operator that we were on the second floor of the old Science building at Queens and that Detective David Tudor had shot my friend. Before I could tell them that he was linked to the murders in Locklyn, Maren motioned for me to end the call.

"What is it?" I asked her.

"He's knocked out cold for now, but he's not dead. You need to find Molly and Elijah. We don't know who The Artist is yet, but I bet he's here."

"I don't want to leave you like this," I answered, as I clenched my jaw to keep from crying.

"It's okay. This is more important. Hand me that cross. I'll hit 'em again if he wakes up."

I slid the cross over to her as I stood.

"Ainsley, take his gun. Make sure it's loaded."

"A gun won't stop the demons," I said.

"No, but it will kill The Artist."

CHAPTER THIRTEEN

I ran down the hall and descended the steps two at a time until I reached the first floor. I hurriedly, but quietly, checked each room on the floor. No sign of Elijah or Molly. I checked my phone. The thirty minutes was up. They should've been back by now.

That only left the basement.

I text Molly. **Where are you? Maren's been shot by Det. Tudor. He's the accomplice.**

Minutes ticked by. Nothing. What-If questions bombarded my mind again and I pushed them away. I didn't want to think about it, so I shut my eyes and leaned against the wall next to the stairwell door.

I cleared my mind completely.

Detective Tudor did send those messages to Alec. More than likely, Alec had called him last night and told him about the artwork. My guess was Detective Tudor met with Alec and somehow convinced him to come to the campus. Maybe to confront Declan or get the framed piece as evidence. A fight ensued, but between who? Alec and Declan? From the look of Detective Tudor's face, he must have been in the fight too. Perhaps, he and Declan teamed up against the highly-trained Alec. Then again,

Detective Tudor's face was fine this morning. He must have fought someone today.

If that was true, then Alec might be dead.

I opened my eyes. I couldn't dwell on that. Not yet.

The hallway began to shift, and I braced myself against the wall as the ripple of energy tore through the corridor and then pulled back onto itself to the stairwell door beside me. I placed my hand on the cold metal door. The electrical current sped through my arm and into my collarbone again. I gritted my teeth through the pain. The Muladach were in the basement, I was sure of it. And if the demons were here, then so was The Artist. I rechecked Detective Tudor's gun to make sure the safety was off. Declan was still unaccounted for and it was getting dark outside.

I needed to find Molly and Elijah.

~ ~ ~

I descended the stairs silently and stopped at the single basement door. I placed my nose against the glass, but I could barely see anything in the dark. I felt for the door handle and pressed it. The door opened with a loud click that made me jump and bite my lip. The basement was eerily quiet with no sign of Molly or Elijah.

I flipped my phone onto the flashlight app and shone it down the dark hall as I followed the wall. I pressed my ear against the locked doors as I came to them, but everything was silent.

Then it wasn't.

All at once, screams of agony carried down the hall towards me. My first instinct was to back away and run, but I caught myself. The screams paused and then a whimpering sound. The screams had sounded like a man. Elijah?

Alec?

I hurried toward the sounds with a lump in my throat.

Oh God, don't let me be too late. Help me end this nightmare.

I stopped at a door near the end of the hall and shone my light on the plaque. Prillerman Auditorium. I slid my phone into my back pocket, so I could use my left hand to open the door. I kept Detective Tudor's gun at the ready.

There was no way the killer could hear me entering the room over the muffled howls, but I slipped in and crouched on the floor anyway. I was in a narrow hallway that opened to the auditorium. The room was illuminated from lights around the corner. From this spot, I could see the chairs facing the front, but the sounds came from the other side of the wall, from the stage.

I stood up and pressed my body against the wall as I inched down to the corner. I could hear the sizzling of acid when the man would stop to take a ragged breath.

Taking a deep breath of my own, I peeked around the wall.

Large industrial lamps shone on a table with a man strapped face down. The psycho above him, wearing a black plastic hooded smock and safety glasses, poured small amounts of acid onto the man's back, causing the man to jerk his head up and scream through the duct tape placed over his mouth.

Oh God, it was Alec.

Alec was the man strapped to the table. As I pulled my head back around to the safety of the small hallway, I caught a glimpse of Molly. She was slouched in a chair facing the table. I couldn't tell if she was unconscious – or something far worse.

I wrapped my free hand around Dad's medallion and closed my eyes.

Then I stepped out from around the corner and raised the gun up until it was level with The Artist's torso.

"Get away from him!" I yelled, as I continued around the front of the stage. The pouring stopped, but the man didn't move away from Alec.

I let go of Dad's necklace and held the gun in both hands. "I said get away from him."

Alec turned his head towards me and tried to say something through the duct tape. It was muffled, but I was pretty sure, he'd ordered me to get out, to run. I shook my head. He would have to be angry with me. I could live with that. I needed to keep him alive until the police arrived. I reverted my eyes back to The Artist, who'd set the bottle of acid and a scalpel down on the counter behind him.

"The police are on their way."

"The police were supposed to have already taken care of you," the man growled, as he removed his safety glasses and then unzipped his smock.

Elijah Moore tossed both onto the floor.

"This was supposed to be my Final Masterpiece. People all over the world would've known my name after I finished it. Can't you see it, Ainsley? How beautiful it would have been? You already liked the image, now it would've lasted an eternity instead of rotting in the ground with the rest of his flesh. My brother didn't have the strength to fulfill his purpose in this life, so his Muladach chose me to collaborate with others to create the art. This work on your friend's back symbolizes his inner demons, and with my help, I'm going to set them free."

I glanced at Alec's face, full of blood, sweat, and tears. "Your other victims, your "collaborators", weren't hurt like this. You were able to perform your work without violence. What changed?" I asked. If I could only stall Elijah until the police arrived.

Elijah smiled as he walked around the table towards me. Alec struggled against the zip ties that bound his wrists to the table.

"That thing around your neck," he said, as he stopped three feet from the gun. "The Muladach whispers to the chosen ones and they come quietly to me. I can remove their tattoos and help them get into position before they take their final breath. The demons tried to bring me Alec, but they told me you'd placed a blessed object on him. He was protected. I didn't know how to get to him. Not until the demons told me about David. He brought him to me, convinced Alec that Declan was the killer. Imagine that, Declan as The Artist," Elijah said, as he smirked.

"Where is Declan?" I asked, afraid to take my eyes off Elijah to look around the room.

"I'm sure they'll find him soon enough. Last night, David texted me that Alec and he were on their way here to confront Declan. Unfortunately, that British fool had figured out I was The Artist after he took apart my *Ainsley* piece. The chaos that ensued when the detectives arrived was unreal. You should've never given him my gift to you."

He turned towards Alec and raised his hand to his head in a military salute. "I have to hand it to you. You were not easy to get. Then again, it takes hard work to create something everlasting."

Alec said something through the tape. Sounded like two words, the second one was probably *you.*

Elijah smirked again. "So, what now, Ainsley? You haven't even checked on your friend Molly over there. Poor girl. Now her, I really liked. You should've seen the look on her face when I slid my pocket knife into her side."

I gasped as I glanced at Molly. I could hear the sirens from the police cars finally. If she could just hold on…

An enormous blow knocked me backwards and into the front seats. Elijah had tackled me. He knocked the gun out of my hand as he grabbed my hair and slung me on the floor with such force, I slid into the table holding Alec, knocking it over onto its side. To be a much smaller man than Alec or Declan, Elijah was strong.

As Elijah reached for me, I jumped away from him and ran straight for the front seats again. I needed to get the gun, but he was right on my heels, clearly in better shape than me. I was able to wrap my fingers around the hand grip of the gun before I felt Elijah's fingers grab my hair at the roots and pull.

As he turned me to face him, I buried the muzzle of the gun into his left shoulder and squeezed the trigger. The sound was still deafening, but Elijah let go of me and fell backwards. He moaned in pain as he rolled on the floor.

I didn't waste a second. I ran to the countertop and grabbed the scalpel before dropping to my knees in front of Alec's face. His back was bloody and raw with chemical burns around the edges of his tattoo. Thank God, he was still alive. I laid the gun down as I pulled the duct tape from his mouth.

"Where is he?" he whispered.

"Over there," I answered, as I cut the plastic ties holding Alec's bloody wrists. Elijah had grown strangely quiet. I crawled quickly to Alec's feet to release them as he twisted his upper body to the floor when a fist came out of nowhere and caught me on the cheek. I crumpled on the cold tile with my hand on my jaw, sure that Elijah had broken every bone in my face.

The man pushed me further down and sat on top of me as he wrestled the scalpel out of my hands. It was as if he'd gotten a second wind. He grabbed my throat with his left hand as he raised his right with the scalpel aimed at my heart. I screamed as a gunshot rang out in the auditorium.

Elijah pitched forward with an expression of surprise on his face.

I pushed him off me to see Alec sitting on the floor, holding Detective Tudor's sidearm. Both of Alec's feet were still bound to the table, but he'd managed to turn it and shoot Elijah in the back.

I snatched the scalpel from Elijah's grip and handed it to Alec to free himself as the room rippled with that familiar supernatural energy again. Standing near the unmoving body of my BFF were the two demons. The two who'd influenced Elijah to take the lives of four people, maybe five, if he'd succeeded with Molly. The same demons who used Elijah to whisper fame and deadly ambition to Detective Tudor.

I slowly stood as I pulled the sleeve up on my shirt. The creatures watched me while bearing their teeth and dripping saliva onto the floor.

Alec hobbled over to me. "What is it?"

"Two of them," I answered. I gripped Dad's pendant with my right hand as I lifted my left forearm in front of me. I took two steps forward.

"*Et adorabunt in conspectus Domini magna ego sum qui misit me. Et revertetur ad inferos.*"

The demons growled at me as they both leaned backwards onto their haunches.

"*Et qui me misit mecum dedit potestatem et auctoritatem vincat. Nunc vadam.*"

The Muladach whined and then let out a howl before they vanished. I grabbed Alec and hugged him tight to me, careful not to touch his back as he buried his face into my hair.

"We need to see about Molly," he said, as he pulled away, but before he could reach her the police burst into the room in a spectacular display of chaos. Alec barked back who he was and rattled off some identification number as the police instructed us to get down on our knees. Apparently, with a dead man only a few feet away and a wounded detective upstairs, no one knew yet who to trust.

But I did, as I brought Dad's pendant up to my lips and sent a silent heartfelt prayer to Heaven above.

CHAPTER FOURTEEN

I sat by Molly's bedside for two days as she hovered in a coma. She'd lost a great deal of blood from Elijah's attack and slipped into unconsciousness. The doctors worked on her day and night and all I could do was sit and pray. I was thankful that Dr. and Mrs. Hiroto allowed me to stay. Unbelievably, and graciously, with everything that had happened with The Artist and Detective Tudor, they didn't blame me.

"Hey," Alec said, as he came into Molly's hospital room carrying two large coffees from the shop downstairs. "I brought your favorite nonfat pumpkin spice latte."

"Thanks," I said, as he handed me the cup. "Except I never told you it was my favorite."

"I guessed," he replied, as he nodded towards Molly. "How's she doing today?"

"The same. I'm worried that this is too much like what happened to Dad."

Alec rubbed my shoulder as he took a sip of his coffee. "Where are her parents?"

"Dr. Hiroto went to the cafeteria to get something to eat, and we finally talked Mrs. Hiroto into going home to rest for a few hours."

"I stopped by the station on my way here," Alec said, as he crossed to the opposite side of Molly's bed and sat down in the oversized recliner, careful not to lean back. "It's abuzz about Molly. We took up a collection for flowers. They'll probably be delivered today."

I tried to take a drink of my latte, but it was still too hot. "How is your back?"

"Sore. It's hard to put the burn cream on and bandage it. It's scarring."

"I'm sorry," I said. "If anything, I can help you with the bandages."

Alec gave me a sly smile. "Hmmm. Have you talked to Maren?"

"Yesterday evening. The doctors told her it was a clean shot. Surprisingly, Detective Tudor didn't hit any major organs and the paramedics got to her in time. They let her go home yesterday, but she's off work for a few weeks. I told her I'd stop by this evening."

"That's good news. David wasn't the best shooter, but he was an okay-shot. I still can't believe I fell for his story about Declan O'Hara. That boy was in total shock when we rolled up into his apartment, guns drawn. David said we weren't waiting on a search warrant since we viewed the evidence sent to you as a threat. I should've waited. I was angry that he'd sent it to you…"

"And it was really Elijah and David's way of trapping you and getting rid of Declan all at the same time," I added, when Alec trailed off.

"He shot that boy in cold blood. All that talent, gone. He didn't deserve that."

"No, Declan didn't. You didn't deserve what they did to you either."

Alec played with his watch for a moment before meeting my gaze again. "Well, it's a good thing my superhero arrived when she did. Anymore, and I think I would've passed out from the pain."

We sat in silence for a little while as we watched the rise and fall of Molly's chest and listened to the rhythm of the breathing machine. It was hard to stay upbeat. The doctors assured us that as soon as they felt she was stable enough, they would try to remove the ventilator and see how she would do. My worst fear, other than the obvious, was that Molly would wake up and never be the same again. Her vibrant and tough-as-nails soul gone.

"Are you ever going to tell me what happened in Wilmington?" I suddenly asked Alec. Detective Tudor had used that as a reason to suspect Alec in the murders.

Alec stiffened in the chair. "Why is that important?"

"It's important to me. The police indicated that you're capable of violence based on what happened there."

Alec ran his tongue over his bottom lip as he stared hard at Molly's blanket. "I will tell you in time. I promise." He met my gaze. "Just believe me when I say I could never hurt you. But I will do whatever it takes to stop someone from bringing you harm."

I swallowed hard as I watched Alec's jaw clench as he spoke. I felt safe with him, but admittedly, there was a fierceness behind those green eyes. Something out of my control - and maybe out of his.

My phone buzzed and I let out a breath I hadn't realized I was holding in. "Hi, Mom."

"Hey, are you still at the hospital?" Mom asked. After what had happened, she was back to keeping a close eye on me.

"Yes. Dr. Hiroto is in the cafeteria and Molly's mother went home to rest. Alec brought me a latte," I answered, as I smiled at him but he didn't see it. He was staring off into space.

"Good. How's Molly?"

"The same," I answered her, as I carefully took the first sip of my drink. "Don't forget I told Ms. Bell I would stop by and visit her this evening. She's doing better now."

"I remember. Do you need me to drop you off?" Mom asked.

"Just a second," I said. I held the phone away from my face. "Do you want to go to Maren's with me this evening?"

"Sure. I'll get us something to eat first," Alec replied with a smile.

"Mom, Alec is going to go with me and then he'll drop me off at home afterwards, okay?" I asked both of them at the same time, since I'd assumed, he would take me home. Alec nodded and threw me his wink.

"Okay, that's fine," Mom answered. "You two be careful. If anything changes, you call me."

After the call with Mom, Alec stretched in the chair and then winced from the pain. "I think your mother realizes that neither one of us would go through torture and near-death for each other unless we had something special between us. Something we're still trying to figure out."

I wasn't sure what that something was either, but I would've gone to Hell and back to save Alec from Elijah and the Muladach. I stood up to stretch and leaned over Molly. If only she'd open her eyes.

I'd sat for so long that my legs ached. After watching me stretch with that look in his eye I'd wanted to see for so long, Alec motioned me over. When I did, he interlaced his fingers in mine and pulled me into the recliner with him as he eased us against it. I laid my head on his shoulder as we held each other in silence and watched Molly's machine breathe for her.

~ ~ ~

After a quick stop at Olive Garden, Alec and I pulled up in front of Maren's townhome. We'd eaten dinner at the restaurant, but I wanted to surprise her with a carry-out order. I told Alec I would pay him back as soon as I started officially working for Henry. Since everything that had happened in Charlotte, Henry decided it would probably be best if I waited until the middle of next week to start the receptionist position.

"You don't have to pay me back. It can be from both of us," Alec said, as we walked up to Maren's door.

I pressed her doorbell before leaning in close to him. "You're still on unpaid suspension. Plus, paying you back might be fun," I answered, and this time, gave him the wink.

Alec opened his mouth to say something when Maren opened the door and invited us inside. She was delighted over her bowl of baked ziti and we followed her into the living room.

"Have a seat. Can I get you anything to drink? Water? Soda?" Maren asked, as she slipped into the kitchen.

"Oh no, I'm good. Thanks," I answered her.

She came back with bottles of water for us anyway.

Alec and I settled onto her couch together as Maren sat in her overstuffed chair and carefully removed the lid to her pasta. "I take it Molly is still the same?"

I nodded. "The doctors are going to try to remove her breathing tube tomorrow and see if she'll breathe on her own. They've been reducing the levels, albeit slowly. I plan to spend the day there."

"Of course," Maren said. "I'll stop by tomorrow too. I feel responsible for her. I should've made her stay here in Locklyn while we went. She wasn't prepared to face something so evil."

"No one realized it was Elijah until it was too late, including me," Alec insisted.

"Don't blame yourself," I replied to her. "You know me, and you know Molly. We were going anyway. We were determined to find them and if you hadn't gone, then I wouldn't have been prepared with Dad's passages." I pulled Dad's pendant out from under my shirt. I'd replaced the chain, but I couldn't let Mom see it. At first glance, she'd probably suspect it was Alec's. However, if she got a closer look, then she would know it was Dad's. There was no way I could explain all of this to her.

"I'm glad to see you wearing Gerry's neck-." The dinging of the doorbell interrupted Maren. She winced as she stood up.

Alec moved quickly to her side. "Do you want me to get the door?"

"Yes, that would help," she answered, as Alec headed for the front door. "I forget I can't just jump up right now," she grumbled to me as she slowly made her way to the front door.

I stood and watched as Alec opened the door wider for Maren. An old priest and another man dressed in blue jeans and a wool coat stood on her porch.

"Father Mahon! Stephen," Maren said. "This is a surprise. You normally call."

"Yes, but I wanted to check on you face-to-face. The discharge nurse told us you'd already left," the older priest said, in a New York accent.

"Please, come in. I want to introduce you to someone," Maren replied, as she and Alec moved away from the door to let the men inside. Maren motioned for me to come over.

"This is Gerald Reynolds's daughter, Ainsley."

The priest removed his black hat and shook my hand. "Ainsley, I knew your father well," he said. He was no taller than me, with white hair that stuck out in tufts from the side of his head. "I see you're wearing his amulet. Maren told us how you bravely stood against the demons and their host. Thank you for using your gift to serve."

"Thank you, but to be honest, I didn't know about any of this until recently. My father kept it hidden from his family." I stared into the older man's kind eyes. He reminded me of someone's grandfather. The type who might sit down and launch into a story at any moment.

The younger dark-haired man stretched out his hand. "Hi, I'm Stephen Reeves. I pastor a small church in West Virginia, just north of Charleston. I was with your dad on a number of investigations," he said, with a twang that matched Maren's.

"Maren told me that he didn't do a lot of them after I was born." Stephen looked as if he might be around Dad's age.

"Not like he used to," he answered, and gave me a sly grin as if he and Dad shared an inside joke.

Maren touched the priest's arm. "And this is Alec Graham, the detective who helped Ainsley. He saved her life."

Father Mahon turned and shook Alec's hand as he narrowed his eyes as if observing something in Alec's face. "Thank you. You remind me a little of Gerald. You have a commanding presence about you."

"Thank you, Father Mahon. It's a pleasure to meet you both." Alec nodded at Stephen.

Maren motioned for the men to sit and I offered the priest a bottle of water. When he refused, Maren enticed him with a cup of coffee which he heartily accepted.

"Stephen, you still take yours the same? Half and half and sugar?" she asked.

"Oh, you know I do, Mare. I'll come help you," he said, as he quickly pulled his coat off and left the room with Maren. He wasn't what I pictured a pastor to look like. I'd always seen preachers in suits on Easter Sunday, but Stephen wore jeans and a black sweater with long sleeves that he'd pushed up to his elbows, showing off a tattoo sleeve. Was it only on his forearm like Alec's or was it full length? From the giggles coming from the kitchen, it sounded like Stephen and Maren went way back. Alec and I smiled at each other. Why couldn't we sneak into another room and giggle like that?

"I'm so glad that both of you are here at this time," the older gentleman said, as he reached for my hand.

I wasn't sure what to do, but the man patted the top of my hand while he spoke. "Seeing you here is not only a bonus, but a sign from The Almighty. You've been chosen to continue Gerald's work here on earth. To scatter the demons and deliver the people from evil."

I slowly slipped my hand away from Father Mahon as I glanced up at Alec who'd turned to face the patio doors. "I'm sorry, Father, but that's not who I am. Trust me, before this I didn't believe in much. Our family only went to church on Easter Sunday. I've seen things now, but I don't know much about the Christian faith. For all that my father helped you, he kept us in the dark. I'm definitely a believer now, but my involvement in all of this supernatural stuff ended when the Muladach vanished."

"The Muladach?" Father Mahon looked confused.

Maren carried his cup of hot coffee into the living room and carefully handed it to the priest. His hands shook slightly as he set it on the coffee table.

"The Muladach is the term coined by the serial killer's brother for the demons," Maren said, as she slipped into her chair. "They tried to influence him first, but it only served to drive him to madness."

"Ah, Muladach," he repeated. "It'd been a while since I'd heard that word. What an odd term to use to describe them. Yet fitting. Madness, sadness, sorrow. All things the demons bring into the world under the veil of humanity. However, the demons may have vanished for a time, but they will return. How many did you see?"

"Two," I answered.

"Just two?" Stephen asked, as he emerged from the kitchen with a large mug in his hand. He stood beside Maren's chair and gave me that inside joke smile again.

The priest chuckled. "My dear girl, there are far more than two in this plane. As a matter of fact, there is, right now, an entire cluster of demons, probably a dozen, at an old plantation home in South Carolina. They are mimicking the sound of children and attracting those who tout themselves as paranormal investigators. There have already been two deaths associated with these "ghosts.""

Alec and I exchanged glances. "I mean no disrespect, but that sounds more like a movie or a book than real life, Father," Alec replied.

"Every good story is rooted in truth, Mr. Graham," Father Mahon answered.

"As a pastor I believed in the supernatural from the get-go, as God Himself is supernatural," Stephen said to Alec. "However, my belief leveled up when I became involved in this with Gerald. The demons are real. The warfare is real. And people are dying every day because either they are influenced or totally possessed by them. Murders, suicides, mass killings.

Of course, some people are to blame, sick people. But, others, you will see, are under an influence."

"Detective Graham, if I were to tell you that you were the only one who could save someone from certain death, what would you do?" Father Mahon asked Alec.

Alec frowned. "I'd learn everything I could about the situation and act accordingly."

"You would risk your life to save the life of another person?"

"Yes," Alec answered. He held the older man's gaze steadily as he crossed the room to stand beside me. "That's why I do what I do."

Father Mahon nodded and then turned to me. "That is what makes up every fiber of Mr. Graham's being. His job is to protect others. But Mr. Graham cannot see the demons. He cannot hear them. That gift was given to you. Yet, the two of you were brought together in such an unlikely and dramatic way. The Seer and the Protector. So, I ask you, Ainsley, what if I were to tell you that *you* were the only one who could save someone from certain death, what would you do?"

I lowered my eyes as Alec placed his hand on my shoulder and gave it a reassuring squeeze.

"I'm not Catholic."

"Neither was your father," the priest answered. "Or Stephen. This isn't about Catholics or Protestants or Jews. Our organization includes many members of different denominations. This is about trusting in God, Your Father who knows your needs, and stopping an insidious evil before more innocent people lose their lives. Saving people like your friend Molly."

I reached up and gripped Alec's hand on my shoulder.

The Seer and the Protector.

"What would you have me do to continue my father's work?" I asked, knowing full-well a trip to South Carolina was in our near future and I still had no idea how to explain any of this to Mom.

THE END

ABOUT THE AUTHOR

Melissa Plantz is an author, Christian, and the founder of Fire and Grace Publishing. As the author of the spiritual warfare devotional series, *Take the Realm*, and of two Christian novels (*Fire and Grace*, *The Muladach*), Melissa is dedicated to equipping today's Christians with the tools for spiritual warfare through the power of storytelling. She believes that it's never been more important to spread the message of Christ, and that maintaining faith in the modern world is a powerful key to fulfillment and happiness.

When not writing, she enjoys spending time with her husband, children, and grandchildren. She currently lives in West Virginia, but she dreams of moving permanently to a beach off the coast of North Carolina. Connect with her at AuthorMelissaPlantz@fireandgracepublishing.com

For more information visit: FireandGracePublishing.com